Christmas Calamity

The Painted Lady Inn Mysteries

By

M. K. Scott

Published by The Sleeping Dragon Press

Copyright © 2016 M. K. Scott
Print Edition

Cover Design by Anya Kelleye Designs.
AnyaKelleye.com

Chapter One

THE NINE-FOOT BLUE SPRUCE wiped out an ornamental planter as Donna pushed at the cut end of the trunk. The dull clunk of the concrete planter explosion made her grit her teeth. Whose idea was it to have an old-fashioned Victorian Christmas? Oh yeah, right, hers.

Her sister-in-law's voice penetrated the branches. "Why did you stop pushing?"

A variety of answers crowded her head with number one being the stupid tree didn't fit. It had to fit. The front door boasted the largest clearance possible in the house. There had to have been past holiday celebrations at the inn. It was hard to imagine one without a stately decorated tree presiding over the festive event.

"Morning, Donna."

The greeting had her abandoning her hold on the fragrant trunk to wave to the dog walkers. "Good morning to you." Great. Everyone would get to witness her very public battle with the evergreen. It also meant they'd witness her failure to push it through. The possibility had her grabbing the trunk, hoisting it up in a battering ram manner, and putting her weight behind it. The tree yielded under her weight and moved another foot until the wide bottom limbs caught on the door. The sound of a muttered complaint reached her.

"I wasn't ready. The vase you replaced that the guest took out

1

almost needed another replacement." Maria's voice carried a tinge of weariness.

"Sorry."

Had Donna's oversized holiday plans exhausted her sister-in-law? Besides the inn, Maria had her accounting job and a husband. Maria's burning goal had never been to run a bed and breakfast. Why did Donna expect everyone to have the same determination and unflagging stamina she did when it came to the inn? Lately, her endurance had also flagged, and the prospect of an entire week off from both the inn and her job at the hospital held some attraction. A tropical cruise or just sunning on a white sand beach appealed. *Toasted* might be a better description since as a natural blonde, she only burned.

The cough of a wonky car motor accompanied her apology. The car slowed and turned into the inn parking lot. It almost sounded like Tennyson's rattletrap car, but he was home for the next two weeks. *What now?* Guests weren't to arrive for two days. Any salesperson wanting to sell her everything from satellite television to pest control she'd dealt with the first year of the inn's opening, but there was a good chance with enough prompting from a supervisor they were ready to try again. *Please don't let it be a child selling something. She didn't feel very charitable.* Although, apple-cheeked scouts were seldom old enough to drive.

Tennyson, her sometime live-in helper, stood on the lawn with his head cocked regarding Donna and the part of the tree she'd failed to ram through the door. "Looks like you need a hand."

"Yeah. I could probably use two or three hands." The sight of the young man relaxed her shoulders. The slender male may not have brawn on his side, but he was young. Instead of lending some muscle as she expected, he strolled around the tree, examining it from all angles before offering his opinion.

"Why didn't you get the mesh bag that compresses the limbs?"

Right now, she could see the reason behind such a device, but since leaving home her holiday history involved trees that came out of boxes where the color-coded limbs helped determine assembly. Maria shouted out an answer for her from inside the house.

"Donna didn't want to pay the extra fifteen dollars for the bagging process! Thank goodness we had Daniel's truck. We'd never have been able to strap it to the car."

Even though it was the truth, it made her sound like Ebenezer Scrooge begrudging the poor a few pennies for their holiday. It was far from that. The tree farm people had a racket going. The tree itself was a hundred and twenty dollars. The white pine with the soft, lacy needles she had intended to get was another forty dollars. Before she could come up with some comment about how it was highway robbery, another shopper snapped up the white pine, leaving her to wrestle with the stubborn spruce.

Tennyson vanished for a few minutes and returned with a worn bed sheet. "Let's put the sheet under the tree and wrap it around the bottom branches. If we keep tension on the sheet, we should be able to get the tree inside."

Part of her wanted to make some comment about the viability of wrapping a tree up, but since she'd been making do with her tiny tabletop tree for the last ten years, she kept her lips sealed. The two of them held the fabric taut as Maria backed the tree into the foyer. Success!

Her fingers uncoiled their death grip on the sheet and were on the verge of letting go when Tennyson spoke. "We better hold onto the sheet until we get wherever you want the tree. Otherwise, the branches will explode out like a green-hued ninja."

The colorful ninja would probably knock out a few things on the way, too. "The wedding parlor." She huffed out the words, even though Maria was already guiding the top of the tree in that direction.

Despite the inclusion of the wedding chapel photos and information in both the brochure and website, they'd had no takers to use the chapel. Her sister-in-law thought if they staged a wedding, complete with flowers and an attractive couple, the idea would appeal to people more, believing most couldn't see beyond the bare bridal arch and the molded white chairs.

Legacy hadn't earned its place as a destination wedding locale yet. That, combined with the fact fewer and fewer people were tying the knot, the chapel, so far, was a financial stumble. Still, she could use the space for events if she hid the arch in the storage room. This month the parlor would represent a traditional Victorian Christmas or at least the Americanized fantasy. Her guests would not appreciate the lack of central heating or hot water to simulate the reality of olden days. They'd also probably nix brick dust to thicken their hot chocolate or chalk to whiten their milk. Nope, her guests would expect the tasty renditions of foods made on modern appliances with fresh spices as featured in holiday movies. Everyone knew how authentic movies were.

The three of them positioned the tree near the bay window after wrestling it into a tree stand. At night, the shimmering tree lights would be the perfect accent for her holiday decorating, at least from the outside. *That reminded her.* She needed to get the outside done, and she had an unexpected helper.

"Tennyson." She gave him a huge smile, then tried to tone it down, realizing it would appear suspect. "I thought you went home to spend Christmas with your family."

Even though it would leave her shorthanded, even Donna wasn't Grinch enough to make someone work on Christmas. Only the hospitals, movie theaters, and restaurants did that.

"Yeah, that." He helped Maria move a table that looked awkward with the tree crowding it. Then the two of them tackled a few other items, making Donna wonder if he'd forgotten the question.

Eventually, he stopped, wiping his sweaty brow and shrugged off his jacket. "I was hoping I could stay here and keep an eye on things so you could have a relaxing holiday."

The words all sounded good, almost too good. People always had a motive, good or bad, for their actions. Somehow, she didn't think Tennyson had her peace of mind entirely at heart. "That works. Not many guests. Of course, we still have old Saint Nick, who's working at the local mall, and the older couple, the Dickens, who came to spend the holidays with their newest grandchild."

Maria removed the white Chantilly lace tablecloths from the drum tables and replaced them with red ones. "Maybe their grandbaby is named Virginia or Snowflake."

Tennyson added with a grin, "Jack Frost or Tiny Tim."

"I doubt anyone would call their child Jack Frost, but I did go to high school with a girl named Merry Christmas. They spelled it the same, too. The poor girl hated her name. She couldn't do much about her last name, but her parents could have called her Teresa or Pamela."

Maria groaned. "Holly or Noel would have worked."

It made no sense to Donna, especially when people had nine months to pick out a name, that they still came up with horrible ones. Laney from the maternity ward would sometimes amuse them at lunch with some of the worst names.

"I'm sure she would have loved being called Holly Christmas.

Her middle name could be Jolly."

Maria snorted at the possibility. Tennyson grinned.

"Since Tennyson is here, he can help me with the outside decorations. Maria, go home and get some rest."

"Appreciate it." Her sister-in-law gave her a salute and patted Tennyson's shoulder as she left the room.

The side door closing echoed through the house, proving Maria took Donna's suggestion seriously. *Good.* It wouldn't be a Holly Jolly Christmas if she ran her family ragged.

Tennyson half-turned in the direction of the hall door. "What's wrong with her? It's not even eleven, and she's tuckered." His gaze returned to Donna, who pulled on the tree, convinced it hadn't been centered in the window. "You're still going strong, and you're so much…"

His words trailed off once he realized he might insult his employer, the same person who was letting him hang out here because something was up at home.

"I'm so much what?" Donna knew he was going to say older. Not too surprising since her brother was younger and his wife even more so. In her opinion, Maria merited the label spring chicken since she wasn't even near forty.

"Ah, no, that wasn't it. I meant…" Tennyson's eyes rolled up as he searched for a safe response. Donna waited, suppressing the smirk that tugged at her lips. "Multi-talented," he finally muttered, ending the comment with a breathy sigh.

"I guess I am." She'd allow him that one, especially since she needed his help outside. "We can work on the parlor in the late afternoon. Let's get the outside done. We're having a Christmas Victorian tea, and I have a special banner I need to stretch across the porch, along with the garlands, bows, and wreaths. I also have miles of fairy lights."

"What have I done?" Tennyson sagged against the wall, flung one arm over his eyes, and spoke in a stilted tone. "Woe is me."

The boy would never be an actor. Donna decided to needle him a little to see what would get a child out of his home over the holidays. Everyone knew that's when the best food happened, along with the Christmas specials and all the parties. "You could always go back home."

A spritely knock on the front door interrupted Tennyson's moan. Donna ambled to the door, knowing good and well it was unlocked. No reason for her few personal guests to knock. Everyone she wanted to see came through the back or side doors. Nothing good ever knocked. She stood in front of the door, debating whether to answer it, but whoever it was could see her through the narrow side windows beside the door.

A bearded man attired in a Victorian frock coat and hat stood on her front step. He nodded at her and glanced at a paper in his hand. "Mrs. Marley, I presume."

"You presume wrong."

The man glanced down at a slip of paper. "Ah, I see." He made a smart turn and headed down the street. Donna was tempted to watch and see what house he went to next, but he kept walking. The shadows thrown by the east-side houses eventually swallowed him up.

Tennyson had followed her out into the hall. "Who was that?"

Weird. No one she recognized; that much she knew. Could be one of those costumed Christmas carolers. That would be nice to have at the tea. Her hand still on the doorknob, she swung it open again, hoping to see the frock-coated man. The high-pitched yip of her neighbor's Yorkie rode the air, but no potential Christmas caroler.

"I don't know. Someone looking for the Marley home, I guess. He called me Mrs. Marley. Do you know anyone named Marley who lives in the neighborhood?"

"No, can't think of anyone, except…" He held up his index finger.

Donna turned expectant eyes on him. The younger residents knew all the gossip, although they'd deny it. She knew Tennyson talked to some of them. An odd niggling sensation had settled in at the base of her neck at the peculiar visitor. "Who?"

"Jacob Marley. Ebenezer Scrooge's business partner."

"Really?" Donna rolled her eyes. Here she thought he'd say something pertinent. She gestured to the porch and pulled the door open. Tennyson followed, closing the door after him.

Two large cardboard boxes of fresh evergreen garlands waited on the front porch. A staple gun and a fluorescent tape measure sat on top of one box. She picked up the tape measure. "Here's the plan. We make six-foot garland loops and staple them onto the wooden porch railing. It has to be precise or someone in the neighborhood will tell me I'm bringing the tone of the place down."

A cherry picker truck moved slowly down the street obviously looking for an address. It stopped a few houses past the inn. Two men wearing elf hats hopped out. Tennyson pointed to the men who'd already knocked on the door and were chatting with the owner, who pointed to a ginormous evergreen in the front yard.

"They must be professional tree decorators." He nudged Donna and pointed again as if she hadn't gotten the message the first time. "That's what you need."

Yeah, she did. Donna needed the two thousand to pay the decorators, too. Some worked for as little as $1,400, but that truck was bound to cost. "I got you. I'm set. Let's get to work."

Together they stretched the garland, measured it, stapled it, measured it again, and more often than not unstapled it and tried again. They worked quietly with the occasional "Now" or "Staple this."

When she decided Tennyson had relaxed into his task, she queried him about his avoidance of home. "Soooo…" She stretched out the word and gave him a sideways glance. "…why decide to come back to work over the holidays?"

He gave her an irritated glance that almost made Donna laugh. Yeah, the kid was in a hard place. Since she was his employer, he couldn't blow her off the way he could a friend or relative. Tennyson could tell her it was personal and leave it at that. In her experience, when a nosy question was put out there, people answered. They realized, in hindsight, they didn't have to.

"Ah, it's awkward at home. Too many people and stuff." He shrugged and managed a lopsided grimace.

No wonder he came back to the inn for sanctuary. Tennyson never struck her as a party animal. The soft purr of a well-tuned engine moved closer and stopped in front of the inn. Before she could look, Tennyson announced the visitor.

"Oh, look, it's your mother."

Donna closed her eyes and sighed.

Chapter Two

A MOURNFUL BAY came from the sedan. It was Loralee, the elderly basset Donna had palmed off on her mother, after Detective Mark Taber had dropped the dog off on her. The set-in-her-ways canine came from divorced owners who didn't have time for the past or their dog.

Remember, Mother did take the dog.

"I should go help your mother." Tennyson dropped his strand of garland and scurried to remove the oversize box from Cecilia Tollhouse's very capable arms.

Donna stood with the staple gun in one hand, the garland wrapped around her arm, one foot on the stepladder while the other hovered in the air. The best thing would be to finish the garland before her mother revealed some new kitschy decoration she had just brought. For a woman who managed to put all the other senior citizens in the shade when it came to fashion, her taste ran to the bizarre when it came to seasonal decorations.

Her parent's stacked heel boots beat out a determined march as Tennyson chatted with her mother. It was cute how he adored Cecilia. He regarded her as a sort of glamorous proxy grandmother.

"Donna, you started without me. I told you I wanted to help."

Ah, yes, she knew there was a reason she and Maria headed out to the tree farm before the sun had been up. Her mother balled her hands on her hips to let her know she was displeased at her sneaky, underhanded ways. The petite woman looked so cute in her matching leopard print gloves and hat it was understandable why people, especially men, knocked themselves out trying to help her.

Of course, anyone who had grown up around Cecilia would know the woman was a dynamo. There was little she couldn't do when she set her mind to it, although tasteful seasonal decorating could serve as her personal Waterloo.

Tennyson watched, probably feeling the need to defend his favorite glam-ma. "I was there when she told you. It must have been Thursday. That was over two days ago." He smiled at Cecilia, who patted him on the arm. Next, she'd pull a butterscotch out of her purse and pop it into his mouth.

The boy, who couldn't even remember when his own classes were, managed to recall entire personal conversations. "Thanks for reminding me, Ten. It's all coming back now. Wasn't that the same day I asked you to wash the first-floor windows?"

His smile slipped and then flattened out. "Could be."

Yeah, she knew it was. The same way she knew he hadn't done it yet. Later on, she'd give him a hand, but right now, she had to deal with her mother. "You're so busy with your social life and various fundraising events I didn't want to bother you."

Her mother wagged her index finger in her daughter's direction. "For you, sweetie, I'd drop everything."

Before Donna had a chance to tell her not to, her mother kept talking.

"Except for today. The bigwigs are coming to town. That's why I couldn't get here sooner. I only have time to drop off the darling train I ordered from the shopping channel."

Donna and Daniel had been the frequent victims of her mother's holiday decorating excesses. She would have bet the objects came from some horror warehouse as opposed to some television show. "It doesn't have any of those creepy elves that slip around the house and leave threatening notes for the children?"

"That's so 2010."

Donna, tired of balancing on one foot, stepped down from the ladder. Her hand went up to rub her neck as she considered what other scary decorations her mother had used in the past. "It's not those gnomes with eyes that follow you around, is it?"

Her index finger wagged again. "Those were adorable, but no, not the gnomes." Loralee interrupted the guessing game by baying again. "As much as I'd love to stay and chat, I have to drop the dog off at the groomers before I meet my celebs."

Tennyson asked the question Cecilia was obviously hinting for someone to. "Who are you going to meet?"

"Well." Her mother's lips tipped up, and her eyes glowed with excitement. "Remember that pop star that sings the sad music to all the animal rescue commercials?"

Donna and Ten threw out half a dozen names, but none were the right ones. Her mother shook her head until they desisted. "It's that singer and her husband. They're coming to put on a benefit concert to raise money for the shelter."

She waved and hurried to her car where Loralee hung out the half-open window, drooling on the freshly washed car. Cecilia moved away from the curb and gave a spritely *beep* as she did so.

The grumpy neighbor she'd nicknamed Madame Litigious happened to be in the midst of her morning stroll. Other people might consider it a walk for exercise, but it was more of a fact-finding mission to see what was wrong in the neighborhood. Donna waved, not trusting herself to not accidently use the name she made up for the woman.

Instead of waving back, the woman shook her cane in the direction of Cecilia's car. "Did you see that hoodlum? Noise pollution! We have standards here in Legacy. Do you know her?" She stared at Donna, then Tennyson.

Great. She'd somehow avoided a frivolous lawsuit, up until now. "No, never saw her before," she lied. "She was collecting money for the animal shelter." Tennyson nodded in agreement.

"Typical. There's a no soliciting rule in the neighborhood. If she comes to my door, I'll call the police." She gave an emphatic nod and moved slowly down the street.

Donna abandoned her staple gun and gestured to the box. Ten carried it up the steps. She followed, but once in the house, she closed the door and leaned against it. "Oh my goodness, I didn't trust myself not to laugh in her face, just thinking about my mother walking up to her door only to have the police called on her."

Tennyson put down the box in the hallway. "I thought I was going to lose it when you denied your own mother." He slapped his thigh and gave a hoarse chuckle.

Donna found herself laughing, too. She tried to explain. "I didn't dare say she was my mother. As an unmarried woman, all anyone would have to do is look up the Tollhouses in the Legacy phonebook. There's only three; Daniel, Mother, and me. Once she had her name, she'd push ahead with her court case."

"Why does anyone care? They're always thrown out."

Tennyson had a good point. "Time, inconvenience, and the sliver of a chance a judge might take her seriously. I know you wouldn't want my mother to go to court."

Tennyson chuckled. "I don't know. It might be exactly what the grumpy neighbor needs. Your mother strikes me as someone who can give back as much as she gets and more."

His observation made her give her helper a second glance. Could it be she had underestimated him? "Bring the box into the parlor, and we'll see how bad it is."

"It's only a train. Plenty of Christmas commercials have a model train running around the tree."

"Yeah, but none of those commercials featured a Victorian holiday. A plain metal train could work since I doubt my tea participants would be model train enthusiasts." So far, she had a dozen grandmothers and granddaughters coming. It probably gave the mothers a chance to get out and get some shopping done. "Let's hope it's only a train. I remember the year of the Christmas cats."

"Were they real?" Tennyson bent and carefully placed the box near the tree.

"No, but I wasn't convinced of it at the time. They were these fluffy stuffed animals with red and green bows on them. They were supposed to purr when you petted them." The memory of fake felines had her shaking her head.

"Did they?" Tennyson knelt by the box and pulled open the flaps.

"I think they must have been discounted or something because all they did was growl. Scared our dog so bad he wouldn't enter the living room as long as the cats were there."

Donna cut her eyes to Tennyson, who appeared slightly ill. He squatted beside the box, weaving slightly, and then tumbled backward to the carpet.

"Tennyson." Donna rushed to her helper, who was already pushing himself up to a sitting position. "The cats weren't that terrible, all things considered."

"It's not the cats." He pointed to the box.

Things couldn't get much more ominous that that. "Let's see

how bad it is." Donna knelt beside the box, expecting something to hurl itself out of the container as she peered in. So far, Cecilia had never bought any live Christmas decorations, if she discounted the cactuses.

Bright primary colors caught her eye. Red, blue, yellow, none of them could be part of her tasteful Victorian Christmas. The item appeared to be a doll of some sort. She reached into the box and lifted out a peculiar toy dressed in a blue and yellow jumpsuit with a round white ruffled collar with crazy red hair and a white face. "I think it's a clown."

Tennyson whimpered. "Put it back. Get it out of the house. It's evil!"

Donna turned the clown around. "There's nothing festive about it. Cecilia must have been sent the wrong package."

Tennyson crab walked back to the wall, still staring at the clown. "It's an omen. Whoever gets the clown is doomed. I didn't take it out of the box, so I think I'm free of the curse. Get it out of the house before something horrible happens."

Her first instinct was to tell Tennyson how foolish he was being. Foolish or not, he was trembling. People never chose what they were afraid of. They just were, usually for a variety of reasons. A former NFL linebacker was on the post-surgery floor when he spotted a spider. The man moved so fast all his sutures had to be redone.

"Okay. I'll take it out of the house." Donna carried the clown around the house to the detached garage. She'd have to stack stuff around it to hide it since Tennyson wouldn't enter the garage if he knew it was in there. On the upside, she could explain to her mother there was no way they could use the clown due to Tennyson's phobia. All the same, she couldn't believe her mother had ordered a clown.

When she returned to the house, Tennyson was standing, although he was holding on to the staircase with a tight grip. "Did you burn it?"

"Of course not. We're not allowed to burn things. I happen to know there's an ordinance against that."

He stumbled, but his tight grip on the newel post kept him upright. "To stop the curse, you have to destroy the clown."

Her sympathy limit had stretched as far as it could go today. "Where did you get this ridiculous story?"

"My cousin told me."

"Seriously!" She threw both hands out, trying not to give into what she wanted to say. *Remember, gentle innkeeper.* She kicked the floor twice with her booted foot.

"No, you have to stomp on the floor three times and say, 'Go away. Stay away. I won't come out to play today.'"

A heavy tread on the stairs preceded the guest before he showed up, all dressed in red, with an authentic white beard and jolly manner. "That doesn't sound like a good attitude. Who won't you come out and play with?"

Ah, Santa would calm Tennyson down. Donna knew the man wasn't really Santa, but he was to her. He'd booked for forty-five days, not only to work the local mall, but also to appear in the Christmas parade and at several events. The Chamber of Commerce even footed the inn cost since they were billing all their holiday festivities as having the real Santa.

The man had arrived with several red suits along with some more relaxed red and green checked shirts for his Santa-at-Home shoots. He also raved about anything she cooked, which meant extreme intelligence. With some luck and the lure of food, she might get him to show up for her Victorian tea.

Robert, who insisted on her addressing him as Kris, had guided Tennyson to a chair. "Who won't you come out and play with?"

Instead of answering, Tennyson dug his toe into the carpet, forcing Donna to answer for him. "There was some weird looking clown in a box of Christmas stuff. It reminded him of something from his childhood.

"Oh." Robert coughed twice, then cleared his throat. It could have been an effort not to laugh, but he still managed a low, caring tone. "I understand clowns can be scary."

Tennyson gave a fervent nod. "Not all of them are bad. I always liked Ronald McDonald. It's just that they paint on a happy or sad face, even a tear, when it isn't how they feel at all."

Robert managed to get Tennyson to talk about happier things, such as spring break at Daytona.

"Wow, you couldn't believe how wasted the girls were. It was like they didn't even know anyone was watching them."

Not a conversation she wanted to hear, Donna stepped into the kitchen, wondering if she should rethink her invitation to Santa to come visit the Victorian tea.

Her phone burbled. Her mother's name and face flashed across the screen. Honestly, she didn't really want to talk to her about the clown fallout, but she might as well. "Hello, Mom. What's up with the clown?"

"What are you talking about? I called to see how you liked the train. It plays a variety of holiday favorites including *Grandma Got Run Over by a Reindeer*. It was a hard decision between that and the mermen ornaments."

"There was a clown in the box."

"That's odd. Look again, I ordered a train. I paid for a train. Why would they put a clown in the box? That's not very Christmassy. North Pole Industries was the company name. Check the box again and see if my train is in there."

"I will. Why are you calling? I thought you were off to meet the celebrity whose name you don't know."

"Ha ha. She's late. We're hanging out, waiting. I figured I'd give you a call."

Donna continued talking as she walked into the parlor where Kris and Tennyson conversed about the joys of summer and girls in short shorts. It was all she could do not to roll her eyes. *Excuse me. You're ruining a childhood image of the jolly elf. He wasn't a lecherous elf.*

When she reached into the large box, Tennyson moaned. "Not anything else, I hope."

Her fingers wrapped around the heavy box and lifted it out, hoping it had nothing to do with clowns. Just in case, she used her body as a block. The image on the top of a black train reassured her that it was actually that. Still, it didn't answer the mystery of the clown.

Chapter Three

DONNA KNELT BESIDE the tree to get the full effect of the decorations. The fairy lights twinkled, throwing illumination onto the metal and glass ornaments. Some of the ornaments even glowed due to the reflection. Everything looked perfect, except for one blinking light on the strand.

"Figures." She reached into the tree to retrieve the problem strand. The prickly tree needles scratched, making the soft scotch pine look even better. All she had to do was give the blinking bulb a twist. Her fingers gripped the tiny bulb as she tried to decide if she should twist it to the left or right. *Probably right.* She gave the bulb a small tweak until she heard it click in place.

Success! She stepped back to admire her tree again, but now the lights pulsed madly as if listening to a fast dance beat that only they could hear. "Rats. That's enough to drive anyone crazy. Not all the lights should be blinking since I fiddled with only one strand." When in doubt, pull the plug out and start again. She felt around for the plug while inserting her face into the needles. No wonder she'd stayed with an artificial pre-lit tree. Not sure how the Victorians managed, even without lights.

Donna pushed the plug back in only to have the lights pop on for a second, then pop off. "Not blinking lights again!" Only the lights never came back on. She waited, looked at her watch, and waited some more.

"You've got to be kidding me." She rocked back on her heels and stood up. "Here I thought I'd get a season out of them and I didn't even get six minutes. Your lights are going back to the store." She wasn't too sure if she wanted to buy the same brand of lights, but she refused to be snookered by defective goods.

Twenty minutes later, she had the lights off and thrown in a store bag along with the boxes they came in and the receipt. After two failed attempts, she decided the lights weren't going back into the box they came in. Besides, if she got them in the boxes, they'd be sold to another unsuspecting person. By the time she'd shouldered her coat on and grabbed her purse, Jasper waited at the door, looking up at her with an expectant air. "You're not going. I have no clue how long it will take me to return these lights."

On the way out of town, she regretted her decision to bring Jasper. The traffic stalled, causing her to shift her car into park wondering if she should switch off the ignition. There had to be a wreck on the narrow highway. She couldn't imagine anything else.

A road flare glowed in the distance joined by both police and ambulance lights. Looks like she was right. If only she could get by the wreck without someone ramming her since they were too busy rubbernecking. A man in a fluorescent orange vest was directing traffic. As she slowly inched forward, she recognized Mark Taber. She rolled down her window, hoping to talk to him.

"What's going on?"

Mark looked up at her question while the car behind her had the nerve to honk. The driver probably thought the wrecked car and ambulance demonstrated clearly enough what had happened.

"Keep going. Can't talk." He gestured for her to move. If she didn't get the hint the first time, the truck behind her beeped again. She slowly moved past the emergency vehicles, noting that someone was strapped to a gurney. At least it wasn't fatal. Tragedies around the holidays were the worst.

At the store, Donna exchanged the lights as opposed to asking for a refund after the young sales clerk demonstrated the new ones worked. There was no blinking single bulb either. She'd get home, restring the lights and be done for the day.

COFFEE STREAMED INTO the waiting glass carafe, scenting the kitchen. Donna grinned. Who says a watched coffee pot never brews? The new tree lights were up, which was a major load off her mind, and she'd managed to do it all without her mother to *help*. Thank goodness the woman had an active social calendar. The animal rescue benefit should be good for a couple more days of distraction. Enough time for Donna to get the rest of the inside decorating done.

She poured herself a cup of coffee and sat down on a stool. Three knocks sounded on the back door before it opened. No need to look. She knew it was Mark Taber, the detective she'd met when she found a dead body in her upstairs parlor. Even after the case closed, Mark kept coming by. Some people might label what they had as a relationship, but she wasn't sure since the man came by for coffee, free food, and the opportunity to pick her analytical brain. The last part he'd never admit to, taking any information or deductions, she offered begrudgingly.

"It's me," Mark called out, as if she couldn't figure it out. The rest of her family usually came in the back door without knocking. The detective had started knocking when she commented about him not doing so and scaring her half to death. It hadn't been a remark to shame the man into knocking, but rather a way to have him declare himself or his intentions. It hadn't worked.

"I know," she called back and slipped off the stool. Even though she didn't need to eat anything sweet, she knew Mark would want something. There was some thawed persimmon pudding in the fridge she could offer. The sweet custard pudding was either a hit or a miss with her guests. Those familiar with it gobbled it down and wanted more. The unfamiliar ones took a pass, even refusing to taste the semi-solid concoction.

She placed the pudding on the plate and finished it with a squirt of real whipped cream. It looked delicious. Donna reached for another plate. After all, getting the tree from the farm and into the house had to have burned enough calories to merit one small serving.

"Oh good, coffee," Mark said, as he removed his jacket and gloves.

Donna wrinkled her nose. "Has there been a time when you showed up when there wasn't coffee?"

His eyes rolled up as if thinking. "There was that time when Arnie and Eunice fought over who got to make the coffee."

Mention of the incident surprised a giggle out of her. "Oh, yeah, that. There was coffee, just not much, especially with you wanting to question the guests. So what happened?" She carried the plates to the island as Mark poured his own coffee.

He saw the plates and made an appreciative hum. "Looks good."

"It is good." She nodded in the direction of the pudding. "When have I served you something that wasn't good?"

From his perch on the island stool, he placed one hand across his heart. "You've never served me anything that wasn't delicious."

"Glory be! Truer words were never spoken."

Mark managed not to choke on his sip of coffee, but did cough a little. The bell hanging on the front door jingled at the same moment. Donna's eyes went to the interior kitchen door, wondering who'd entered the foyer. She'd made two steps in the direction of the door when it swung open on its own. Herman, her elderly neighbor, stood in the opening with his parka hood up and a muffler around his neck and chin. The man was more dressed for Antarctica than the slight temperature downswing that would eventually bottom out at forty-nine degrees. People in Alaska would wear shorts, but in Legacy, women who had furs took them out of storage when it hit sixty degrees.

Herman chafed his arms and looked pointedly at the persimmon pudding Mark was currently enjoying. "I wouldn't be averse to a cup of coffee and whatever Mark is eating."

What a surprise. Donna stirred in the two sugars and cream Herman took in his coffee. The gossipy neighbor often dropped by for a visit and provided her with tidbits about the neighborhood. Lately, he timed his visits with Mark's to get the scoop on the local crime beat. Generally, the best the detective could give was tales of youths stealing a six-hundred-pound concrete bear out of someone's yard and then sending a ransom note along with a pic of the blindfolded statue.

Herman held out his hand for the coffee and rewarded her with a smile. Donna grinned back, realizing the nosy neighbor had grown on her. On her hospital days, she missed seeing Herman, Tennyson, and Mark. The long shifts didn't leave her much time to check on the inn, although she did some days. "Have you ever had persimmon pudding?"

"Please, I was raised on it." He waggled his shaggy eyebrows.

He should have recognized it, but Donna decided to not comment, especially in front of Mark. The elderly man wouldn't appreciate her questioning his honesty or his memory. She gave him her piece and cut a much smaller one for herself. People might think she didn't eat her own cooking, but they had no clue how much she consumed during the creation—too much.

Herman wolfed down his pudding, proving he was indeed familiar with it or hadn't eaten yet today. He watched Mark closely as he ate. It reminded her of the way Jasper monitored her food intake, possibly hoping against hope that a morsel might fall to the floor. She was about to offer to get Herman another piece when he spoke.

"Guess you haven't heard about the mob killing on Route 17?"

Mark slammed his coffee cup on the island top, sloshing a bit onto the granite surface. "There was no mob killing." He shot Donna a questioning look she had no trouble interpreting. *Was the man joking?* She shrugged. Normally, Herman would laugh at his own jokes, but his avid expression showed no hint of humor.

It wasn't the usual way to start a conversation, and Donna wanted to know why. "What are you talking about?"

"On 17, someone drove by and shot the driver in the head." Herman held up his index finger. "My old war buddy in Wilmington heard it on the police scanner. He called me since it happened closer to Legacy than Wilmington."

Mark sighed. "I had hoped to come by here for coffee and a moment of peace. I don't need you spreading gossip."

Herman's head jerked back as if slapped as Mark pulled his cell out of his pocket.

He thumbed through his texts before standing. "I better go. Thanks for the treat." He nodded in Donna's direction, pivoted to face Herman, and patted him on the back. "I wouldn't go telling everyone it was a mob hit when it's probably a domestic. They're the worst."

The two of them watched Mark leave. After the door closed,

Herman gave her a sly look. "It was too a mob hit. I know he doesn't want me spreading it around. Wouldn't be good for tourism if people thought *The Family* settled here." The man looked over his shoulders, then at the interior door before whispering. "We can't be too sure the place isn't bugged."

Even though it wasn't her intention to play into his paranoia, she had to ask, "What makes your friend think it was a mob hit?"

"Glad you asked." He pivoted his head to make sure no well-dressed men with suspicious gun bulges under their suit jackets were hiding in any corners. He motioned her closer. "Jeb, my friend, has a great-nephew, Jim Bob. He's not the best hunter, but he was out today, hoping to get a sizable buck. Well, he didn't have any luck and was driving home when he..." Herman hesitated, searching for the right word.

Donna finished his statement for him. "Saw a buck along Route 17 and pulled off to take a shot at him."

Herman grimaced. "I was trying to leave that part out."

"Anyhow..." She gestured with her hand for him to continue.

"He missed. Took three or four shots, but the buck must have dropped to its knees."

Not the part she wanted to hear, but Herman had a method to his stories. Trying to rush him would end up with him starting the story over again. "Jim Bob wasn't drinking, was he?"

The man shot her an incredulous look at her guess. Apparently, the grand-nephew had had a few, probably due to his failure to catch the buck. Deer were so thick in some parts of the route that posted signs warned motorists of the danger. Most people knew all it took to bag a deer was an inattentive driver and a minivan. An SUV would serve in a pinch. "The Mafia hit?"

"Oh, yeah. When Jim Bob walked back toward his truck, an

expensive sedan shot by followed by a motorcycle with two guys on it, dressed in all black, wearing black helmets."

Donna wasn't too sure when the Mafia part entered the tale. "Jim Bob thought the folks on the motorcycle were hitmen because they were wearing black? They could have been from New York or another one of those big cities where they wear black."

"You've got to let me finish my story." He glanced down at his empty plate, then up to Donna with an expectant look.

There'd be no more details until the plate miraculously refilled itself. Donna grabbed his plate and carried it to where the pan of persimmon pudding sat. "I'm only doing this because I like you, not for any details of a story that is probably fabricated."

Herman snorted behind her back. While she might have his number, he probably had hers as well. The man refused to say another word, although his amused expression said enough. Donna squeezed a little extra whipped cream onto the pudding before placing it in front of him.

He dipped his fork into the pudding before resuming his tale. "The part that made him think it was the mob was when the motorcycle came abreast of the sedan, the guy on the back of bike held up a gun and shot through the car window. Jim Bob said it was more of a whine than a bang. Silencer, you know. The car goes out of control and runs off the road. The motorcycle takes off."

If it were a true story, then she'd almost agree with Jim Bob. "What happened then?"

"First, Jim Bob waited a few moments before coming out of the woods. He didn't want to become the mob's next target. He jumped into his truck and drove a few miles, then made an anonymous call from the gas station that an accident had happened on Route 17 and gave them the general coordinates."

Donna wondered about the people in the wrecked car in desperate need of medical assistance and Jim Bob speeding off. Could be he truly was afraid. More likely, he had several outstanding warrants. Then again, if it were a fabricated story, as she assumed it was, she'd just wasted time analyzing it.

"It's the truth." Herman held up his right hand as if testifying. "Don't think I can't see the wheels turning in your head. You're probably thinking Jim Bob drove off because he didn't want to get fined for shooting so close to the highway."

That thought hadn't crossed her mind, but it could be a legitimate issue.

Herman curled the fingers of his raised hand into a fist and thumped it against his chest. "Right after that, you probably thought the old man makes crap up. This is another of his stories, right up there with the diamond heist."

He hit that nail on the head, but Donna refused to acknowledge it, knowing it would offend him. Before she could think of the best thing to say, Tennyson came through the back door, talking.

"Hey. There's been a drive-by shooting on Route 17."

Herman raised his eyebrows and slammed his fist on the counter. "Booyah!" He winced and shook the pounding hand.

People never thought about the counter being granite. Donna rushed to examine Herman's hand. "Wiggle your fingers." He did. Her thumb applied gentle pressure as she surveyed his papery skin for any obvious marks or contusions. "No broken bones, but you'll have a dilly of a bruise. I'll get you a bag of frozen peas to mitigate the swelling."

Tennyson watched the unfolding medical drama before drawing attention back to himself. "Don't you want to know how I heard?"

"How?" Donna asked as she rooted through the upright freezer for a bag of peas.

"Heard it on the police scanner in Santa's truck."

Herman cocked his head, possibly ready to ask what Santa was doing in town so soon, which would probably derail Tennyson's attention. Donna handed her neighbor a bag of peas as she explained. "He means Robert. The man plays Santa down at the local mall. Surely you've seen him leaving in his red suit."

"Yep, I did wonder where he parked his reindeer." He chuckled at his own quip, but no one else did.

Donna prompted Tennyson. "Why were you in Santa's, I mean Robert's, truck?"

"Oh, that." Her employee flushed and looked away. "Um, it was the clown incident. Santa, ah, Robert wanted to cheer me up."

Herman interjected himself into the conversation. "Did he give you some pixie dust?"

Before Donna could correct him, saying pixie dust had to do with Peter Pan, Tennyson answered. "Oh, no, he took me out for a beer."

Her long-term guest was ruining all her well-loved Christmas myths. There was a good chance before the man left, she'd find out the little drummer boy did not go ra-rum-pum-pum-pum. A quick glance revealed it wasn't even noon. "Are you even twenty-one?"

"As of two days ago, but Santa just popped into the grocery and bought a couple cold ones and a nine-pack for later."

Mercy. She did not need a drunken Father Christmas. "He's not still driving, is he?"

Tennyson bobbed his head. "Really, it was only one beer, not even a tall boy. A guy his size can probably put away a great deal and not even feel it."

Donna gave Ten her long *Are you kidding me* gaze that he'd

endured more than once. "That's a common myth people tell themselves to rationalize drinking more. Trust me. I've dealt with enough drunks in the ER. All we need in Legacy is an inebriated Santa to plow into a crowd of children. That would make everyone forget about the drive-by shooting in one second."

Herman waved his good hand for attention. "I still want to hear about the drive-by. It might limit my driving if I know which places should be avoided."

Tennyson shifted his eyes to Donna, and his lips pulled down into a scowl. "You always expect the worst of people. Santa, um, Robert, wasn't going to drink all the beer himself. He was on his way to party with a couple of cute elves he met at the mall."

Elves? Really? It must be code for shop girls with granddaddy issues. Donna exhaled through pursed lips, releasing the toxins out the way the yoga instructor had taught her. She took an internal survey and realized she still felt the same, slightly put out that her guest would have a hankering for liquor and women, which made him pretty much like almost every other man she knew.

"Drive-by." Herman raised his voice. "I'm eighty-two, and I might not make it to eighty-three. I'd like the details about the drive-by before I keel over."

Tennyson stepped over to Herman and awkwardly patted him on his hurt hand, causing him to grimace. "I'm so sorry, but not a whole lot to tell. It came across the scanner that a Mercedes sedan with New York plates crashed on the side of 17. An unknown citizen called it in as a drive-by shooting."

"Thanks," Donna said. "Really, appreciate your help. We're fortunate you got the scoop on it." Especially since Mark hadn't intended to tell her anything.

Both Herman and Tennyson threw her an odd look. Maybe her

praise was a little over the top, but darn it, she felt bad she'd forgotten the boy's birthday. Well, not really forgotten it. She assumed he'd celebrate it at home. She had planned on having a cake and a gift for him when he eventually came back after being away. Showing up early had blasted those plans to smithereens. The weight of their combined stares forced her to say something to break the silence.

"Out-of-state plates means it can't have anything to do with Legacy." Or the inn, she mentally added in relief.

Chapter Four

"**T**OO BAD IT isn't dark yet." Donna narrowed her eyes as she gazed at the fairy lights draped around the evergreen garland. "I know they're on."

Tennyson cautiously stepped off the scaffolding ladder from where he'd carefully placed a light-ring Donna had purchased when she returned the faulty lights. Strings of lights hung down the only decently shaped evergreen in the front yard. "Night comes fast this time of year." He nodded at the tree he'd just crowned. "What should we do with the lights?"

After walking slowly around the tree, she paused and fingered a strand of lights that hung slack against the green boughs. Donna glanced back at the neighbor's decorated trees, but it was hard seeing anything due to the daylight. Still, they probably had their lights looped around the tree, which meant she needed to do something different. Small clips on the light strands would allow her to anchor the lights in straight lines radiating from the top. Not very Victorian. She wrinkled her nose at the image. Of course, Victorians didn't have Christmas lights. Her great-grandmother said her uncle usually stayed home sick from church on Christmas Eve. When they returned the tree would be up, decorated, with all the candles lit.

The candles hadn't been in straight lines either. She took a step back from the tree, put her right hand up in the air and made rocking motions as if drawing sea waves.

Tennyson directed his attention to the street. "There's no one out there unless you're waving to the mail carrier."

"Nope. I'm having an artistic inspiration. We should make the lines come down in curvy lines rather like waves." Yeah, that would be original. "Back up the ladder, we'll need to keep the curves uniform too."

"Not sure what this has to do with an old-fashioned Victorian Christmas." He grumbled something else as he climbed back up the ladder.

She supervised from the ground. "The wave is cresting two inches too soon."

"How can you tell that from down there?" Tennyson had one arm wrapped around the ladder in a death grip.

"Artistic vision."

"Maybe you should be up here instead of me."

Donna forced a laugh since she always kept her fear of falling a secret. "Goodness, no. I'm old. You don't want to put some old lady with wonky balance on a ladder." The fact she'd actually refer to herself as an old lady underscored how deep her fear went. Anyone else saying that would get an elbow straight to the ribs for their effrontery.

"Yeah, whatever."

She managed a sniff, disturbed. He hadn't insisted she wasn't old, but when you're young, everyone over thirty appears ancient. Unfortunately, she understood her mother's comments about her friends cut down in the prime of their life when they died in their fifties. A slight vibration against her chest didn't indicate heart conditions, but her cell phone.

The image of her mother flashed as she turned her phone over. She probably wanted to know Donna's opinion on the train. So far, she hadn't taken it out of the box, but it *was* a train. A plus in her opinion after the clown incident.

"Hello, Mother."

"Oh, Donna, the most horrible thing happened."

With her mother, that could mean anything. The groomers could have done a bad job on Loralee. What could you do wrong to a basset hound? "What?"

"Remember the bigwigs coming to town?"

"The singer, whose name you couldn't remember and her spouse?"

"Yeah, them. They never showed. It's hard to have a fundraiser when the guest of honor isn't there. The good news is no one knew she wasn't going to show so we did have a turnout, but people had to buy tickets in advance. Only two demanded their money back. Twelve dogs were adopted, mainly puppies."

At least Loralee hadn't suffered a traumatic haircut. "It all worked out then."

"Not really. We had to pay the no-show fee for her room at the Regency Deluxe."

Did she hear that right? "You could have booked at the Painted Lady. You chose another place over your daughter's bed and breakfast?"

"Ah, they had a lot of demands."

"Such as?"

"Room service."

"I could do room service and a lot better than that cold congealed crap that passes for food at the Regency."

"Bathrobes?"

"We have bathrobes, much cuter than the cheap terry ones at the other place."

Her mother's heavy sigh carried over the line. The woman had run out of excuses.

"Hetty's daughter manages the Regency. She gave us the employee discount. Would you give us a special cut-rate price?"

That was a hard one. "It is the holiday season." Originally, she thought people would crowd the place during Christmas, but she'd figured wrong. Most stayed at home. The lucky and the few went somewhere closer to the equator or boarded a cruise that at least stopped at a tropical locale. No one ever said, "Let's go to the coast of North Carolina" in the winter. Robert and the Dickens were the notable exceptions.

In her B and B fantasy world, she had raised the price due to it being the holidays. "No, I probably wouldn't have gone for the discount."

"There you go. I did you a favor by not asking."

A figurative light bulb glowed above Donna's head. "If the unnamed celebrity was really famous, I might change my mind about the discount and could let it discreetly slip after her visit that she'd stayed here." People would flock to the place just to be where she stayed. Anxious fans would request the same room. "Having a known celebrity stay here could be good business. It would have to be the right kind of person, though. Not someone known for destroying hotel rooms or biting the heads off chickens. One of those nice morning show hosts, even a former president, or Miss America. You don't plan on inviting any of those types to your next gala?"

Her mother's familiar tinkling laugh carried over the phone. "First, we can't invite particular people to boost your inn's reputation. Second, we approached almost sixty animal-loving celebs to get this one gal and even she didn't show. Mary Lou Gaither is second cousins to the guy up in Ohio who has that animal show, but he wouldn't come. He was honest and told us no as opposed to yes, then not showing up."

"I'm sorry. In the end, you still raised money, and the pets were adopted. It worked out."

"Yes." Her mother managed to put her resignation in that one word. "Tori, the vice president of the shelter, thought if we'd popped for airfare that our celeb would be here. Airfare for her and her husband would have made a huge dent in any money we raised. It could be they started driving from New York and decided the trip was too long. Still, the woman had insisted on driving."

Couldn't have been that big of a celeb if she answered her phone and managed her own promotional ops. Any diva would have demanded a plane and first-class airfare as well as dragging along a retinue of lackeys. "What if they're still on their way? Traffic, road construction, even a wreck could have delayed them. Could you manage to throw something together if she shows?"

"Always!" The upswing in Cecilia's voice signaled a definite mood shift. "I need to go and contact the other volunteers about this great possibility."

Her mother hung up without even telling her goodbye. Donna sucked in her lips, knowing she'd planted false hope where none existed, but it bothered her to see her normally effervescent mother feeling blue. Most people tiptoed around Cecilia, never wanting to see her sad. Back when the Cabbage Patch dolls came out, her mother had turned into a determined dynamo as she sought out one of the coveted dolls for her daughter.

At the grand age of twelve, a soft body doll with yarn hair was the last thing she wanted for Christmas. Her wish list included music albums by teen heartthrobs, clothes, a makeup case with actual makeup, and a cute fedora similar to one worn by a popular teen celebrity. Instead, her mother got her a boy Cabbage Patch doll.

On Christmas Day, no one was more excited than her mother. Before Daniel and she ripped into their presents, her father always whispered into her ear to act thrilled, no matter what. Obviously, he knew about the doll, but couldn't dissuade his wife from getting the hot new toy. Her acting job must have passed muster. Eventually, everything she did want would mysteriously appear in her room one by one, even the makeup kit. That arrived only after her father drove her to a mall and stood awkwardly in the middle of the cosmetic section of a high-end anchor store as a woman in a white lab coat taught her how to use cover-up and foundation.

Donna had washed off her skillfully applied makeup and hid the case. If her mother found out her father did all this behind her back, things would be tense. Instead, she complimented her mother on her makeup and asked if she'd teach her how to wear it. As fate would have it, Cecilia drove her to the same store for a makeover. The same woman with the penciled-in eyebrows did the makeover. At the time, she tried to give her a significant look that said *Be Cool. Say Nothing.* Later, she realized the woman probably couldn't tell one prepubescent girl from another. It demonstrated the lengths her father would go to not to upset her mother.

Outside the windows, the daylight diminished as the shadows grew. *Good.* It would allow her to test out the lights. With any luck, they would all work. The last thing she wanted to do was return more lights.

It would help when she had the lights on the Christmas tree, and its festive glow added to her holiday tableau. Clear icicle lights dripping from the porch gutters would have been nice. The price and length of the porch discouraged that. Maybe next year, after she had a famous celebrity stay at the inn, which would result in major bookings.

A quick glance around revealed Tennyson was nowhere in sight to help. She'd given him two weeks off, so it seemed rather unfair to ask him to help. Still, if he expected to stay and be paid, it wouldn't kill him to help.

Some festive music might bring him out of wherever he was. Her faux Santa was off partying with Legacy's less desirable denizens, while the Dickens were spending quality time with their grandson. No wonder the place felt so empty. A mellow voice poured out of the speaker, reminding her that it was cold outside. Even though no one could use winter in Legacy as a reason for staying a little bit longer, she decided to make hot chocolate and pull out the sugar cookies she painstakingly decorated with raisin eyes and red hot mouths. Colored sugar and icing completed the rest of their elves' attire.

As the milk heated, she knocked on Tennyson's door. "I have cookies and hot chocolate if you're interested." It never hurt to use food as a lure.

A drowsy voice answered her. "Okay. Be right there."

It explained where he had been. "I thought we'd have it in the parlor since it would be more festive." No need to mention her intentions since the best way to convince someone was to let them think it was their idea.

Donna pulled out the shopping bags full of garland and extra ornaments she purchased when returning the lights. Authentic ornaments would have been small cakes and candies, but Christmas trees didn't stay up for a month in Victorian times. Delicate glass creations that resembled yummy treats and hard candy would serve similar to the lights standing in for the candles. She'd also read that the early trees were decorated with realistic small dolls with human hair hiding in the branches that were intended gifts for younger girls. She'd pass on that one. It struck her as creepy, rather like the clown.

By the time she'd gone back for the hot chocolate and cookies, Tennyson emerged from his room. His disheveled hair and wrinkled clothes testified to his latest activity along with his slightly groggy manner. If he were feeling better, Donna might have joked about him acting like a zombie, but not today.

Her chances didn't look that good at getting him to decorate. "Let's go in the parlor. I've loaded the CD player with all my seasonal tunes. There's 'Holly Jolly Christmas,' 'White Christmas,' 'Frosty the Snowman,' 'Rudolph,' and of course, 'Grandma Got Run Over by a Reindeer.'" She waited for the expected groans, but none came.

"I'm not familiar with them." Tennyson shook his head and started again. "What I mean is, I've heard them before, but not that much. My mother tried to stop Christmas."

"Say what?" Surely she misheard him. A person might as well try to stop the sun from shining. "Is it a religious thing?"

"Not really. My mother is Catholic, but she and God aren't on speaking terms due to my granddad dying before his time." He accepted the hot chocolate Donna handed him and took a sip before continuing. "Yep, I wasn't born yet, but my sister was ten. She remembers. Missy calls it the day all the good holidays died. We couldn't do Easter, either."

Most of the time, Donna had an answer or an opinion for every situation, but not this one. The thought of a tiny Tennyson missing a tooth with no stocking or ornament with his name on it almost broke her heart. All this over-the-top decorating probably sickened him. No wonder he was in his room, probably crying.

"Ah." She held her fist up to her mouth, not sure how to back-pedal. A childish voice sang in the background about wanting two front teeth. The room smelled of cinnamon and apple potpourri and felt very warm. "I was going to ask you to help me finish decorating the tree, but now I realize you wouldn't want to."

Tennyson put down his mug on the tray and wiped the marsh-mallow froth from his lips with the sleeve of his shirt. "I'd love to decorate the tree. It will be my first."

The two of them circled the tree hanging glass candies along with silver angels simply because Donna liked angels. Tennyson readily spoke of growing up without a December celebration. "In my first-grade class, I was the kid that celebrated nothing. The other kids were encouraged to share their holiday traditions. Kenny explained Hanukkah and even brought in a menorah. J'male brought in something her mother had baked for Kwanzaa. Even Rowan brought in holly and oak leaves and told us about the Holly King replacing the Oak King at Yule. When it came to me, I told them my mother wouldn't let us watch television most of the month of December because she didn't want us to see any Christmas specials or commercials. Before I could say more, my teacher cut me off. I had no clue I was ruining it for other kids."

"Surely you had to have some exposure to the holiday. How can you avoid it when some stores are putting out decorations as early as August?" Donna carefully moved an ornament that wasn't the right distance from the other ornaments. Originally, she thought Tennyson's parents to be kind, decent people, but now she wasn't so sure. It also explained why a drinking Santa who ogled girls wasn't an oddity in Ten's world.

"Technically, I couldn't. A sighting of a red stocking or an over-sized plastic cane became my porn. I'd often get lost while shopping with my mother so I could dash through the holiday furnishing. Sometimes, I'd squeeze in between the lighted Christmas trees, close my eyes, and then open them slowly. It was magical. For a brief second, I could pretend my life wasn't that different from anyone else's. I even checked out *A Christmas Carol* and read it under the blankets with a flashlight."

Her heart hurt. It was all she could do not to call up his mother and give her a good tongue-lashing. "What about you mentioning Jack Frost or Tiny Tim? Pretty good for a fellow who knows nothing about Christmas."

"Ah, that." He chuckled. "That was me trying to fit in with my peers. I learned fast that not celebrating, no matter if you went to church or tore open gifts, made you weirder than having one eye. Besides, it was easy to research on the school computers. I'm sure the librarian was glad I was looking up holiday traditions and not hot girls."

"I can imagine." She presented the plate of cookies to Tennyson who picked out an iced bell. "Did you decide to go into philosophy due to not having any family holiday traditions?"

Tennyson stopped in the middle of placing a tiny wrapped package on the evergreen branch. He cocked his head and stared off into the distance. His words came slowly. "I always thought it was the clown that caused my choice, but maybe the lack of Santa figured into it, too."

Chapter Five

THE FAIRY LIGHTS twinkled against the night, creating small areas of illumination on the evergreen garland and red velvet bows. The chilled night air carried the scent of pine and wood fires. The sound of voices and car doors announced the neighbors had guests and were possibly hosting parties. Donna and Tennyson stood side by side, gazing at the effect of their day spent decorating. The oversized Christmas tree sparkled in the long parlor window.

Never a fan of the cold and not all that thrilled with the outdoors, Jasper nudged her hand. "Just wait, buddy. Do you think I should have gone with clear lights for the inside tree?"

"No. I think the colored lights make it look happy. Everyone should be happy at Christmas."

If it were only that simple. Donna had worked the last twenty-two Christmases of her life and would probably work this year. It only seemed fair. Other people had a family. When she worked, it gave them the opportunity to spend the morning together, unwrapping presents. "I like to think everyone is happy even when I know better. Spend the holiday in the ER and you'll find plenty of reasons to believe it's a charade, no more than a costume people don by mutual agreement on December 24, only to rip it off on the 26th or sooner."

Tennyson turned in the darkness. "Now you're starting to sound like one of my professors. Let's go finish the tree and the cookies."

The three of them strolled in together, much to Jasper's relief. He ran into the kitchen to inspect his bowl. Donna followed. "Okay, buddy, I'll give you a treat, but keep in mind you did nothing to deserve it." Since they were still decorating the tree, another round of hot chocolate was in order. After all, this was Tennyson's only experience with normal holiday traditions.

Cocoa ready, she placed it on a tray and carried it into the parlor. The boy who missed Christmas decorated the tree with a smile. Ah, it did her heart good. "So, how's your first official Christmas?"

"It's not my first. I will admit to dating a girl I felt nothing for through December to experience the entirety of the holiday. Just my luck, she called it a bunch of crass commercial nonsense that she refused to have anything to do with, but her family still had the tree and everything." He bit into his cookie and chewed.

She understood the girl's defensive technique. She may have even used it a time or two herself. "Did you make the mistake of not getting her a gift?" she asked, already knowing the answer.

He did a double take and then swayed side to side while asking, "Hey, do you know Sharona?"

"Ah, no, but I do know a thing or two about women. Gift giving is an important and tricky business. Even if she said she didn't want a present, she did. You could have bought her something she didn't want and also make sure it was quality and not too cheap. Nothing you picked up at a gas station or a discount store on your way over. As a money-strapped student, you could have even made her something."

Donna always preferred to keep any dating activity a secret to keep her family from getting their hopes up, not that there'd been that much. Those who made the dreaded drugstore run by for her birthday or Christmas were history.

"I don't get it." Tennyson stopped his swaying, reached for a cookie, and bit into it. He spoke while chewing, causing a few crumbs to expel with his words. "How would it be better if I got her an expensive gift she didn't like?"

She reached for a cookie herself, picking over them to find the smallest one, the holly leaf. Even though she made delicious desserts all the time, sugar cookies were her weakness. If she didn't pace herself, Santa would be putting larger clothes under the tree, which would make her mad at the jolly old elf and herself. "The act of gift giving proves to a female that she's important in your life."

"She wasn't." He blinked, probably baffled about the gift-giving etiquette when it came to women.

"I think she got that message, which is why she was mad." Donna inhaled deeply. Why did so few men understand the importance of getting the right gift to demonstrate their affection? Something too expensive meant a commitment the woman might not feel. Too sexy implied a level the female might not appreciate either. Too cheap, well, that said more about the man. "Consider that her friends and relatives would ask her what you got her. Every time she told them nothing, it would remind her that you thought she wasn't important. Each time she'd get a little madder."

"Ah, I think I understand."

Donna smirked. "Then you're better off than most of the male population. Did she get you a gift?" It was always worse if the woman put time and thought into the perfect present, and the man did nothing in return.

"Yeah, a T-shirt. One of my favorites actually. It's the *You Can't Make a Good Deal with a Bad Person* one."

It was an honest saying that most guests wouldn't be offended by since no one ever thought they were the bad person. Donna left it alone when she did her laundry cull. The more offensive shirts she replaced with plain shirts of the same color, swearing the high-heat dryer melted off the words. Tennyson never questioned her. "You kept it?" Her voice grew tight in surprise.

"Why not?"

All she could do was shake her head and sigh. The gift-giving training of men had to start much earlier. "My father was a wonderful gift giver." The front door bell jingled, stopping Donna in mid-thought. The door remained unlocked until 10 p.m. when there were guests around. She stretched her neck a little, hearing the sharp sound of heels on the wood floor, before the oriental runner softened them. The clatter of dog nails hinted at who the new arrival might be.

"My father not only bought us exactly the right thing, he also gave my mother fabulous gifts. Not sure why he was so much better at it than the other men in our neighborhood."

Her mother's voice drifted into the room. Loralee wore a festive neckerchief and plopped down near the glowing fireplace, managing a canine moan. "It's because I trained him. No man is the self-sacrificing husband from *The Gift of the Magi.*"

Tennyson's forehead furrowed. "Huh?"

Donna explained. "It's a story about a turn-of-the-century couple that sell what is most precious to them to buy each other gifts."

His nose crinkled, joining his brow. "Well, that's stupid."

"Donna," her mother said as she angled her head at Tennyson, "we have a great deal of work to do with this one." She peered into their cups. "I'll go make myself some cocoa. I may need to enhance it."

"Remember, the liquor cabinet combination is Dad's birthday."

Anything of value she'd locked up which included liquor, food, even linens after discovering in her first month as an innkeeper that people helped themselves. Now the booking site included a warning that some items taken, including towels or robes, would be added to the bill. She'd never expected anyone to use the linen closet as a personal shopping stop. She never knew who her sheet thief was and couldn't charge anyone. Locks helped.

"I know," her mother answered and left the room in haste.

Tennyson cut his eyes in the direction Cecilia went. "Do you think she's okay?"

"I don't know." Her father's death had hit her mother hard, but in typical Cecilia fashion, after six months of grieving, she threw herself into charity work and surprisingly, dating, although she was quick to explain she just didn't want to go to dinner alone and wasn't looking for a stepfather for her adult children. "It may be that animal shelter fundraiser thing."

At Tennyson's blank expression, she decided to explain. "Some famous singer was driving down from New York with her husband to appear at the fundraiser. She never showed."

Despite Tennyson's uplifted finger, Donna plowed on. "I guess she's upset about that. It's embarrassing, to say the least. Somehow, I'd expect my mother to blame herself."

"Maybe they were the car that got shot at?" Tennyson spoke when Donna paused to take a breath.

Truthfully, since Herman told her the story, she considered it suspect. "Herman or someone mentioned New York plates."

"See." He waved his still uplifted finger. "That would explain why they never arrived. They're probably dead."

The sound of breaking china catapulted Donna into action. Her mother stood slack-jawed, staring at a growing stain amid the dish shards. She ushered her mother to a wing chair she'd moved into the parlor for the holidays. Ideally, it would be for Santa to pose with the pint-sized guests. "Here, sit down."

Tennyson tossed Cecilia a worried look as he dashed past them. "I'll clean up."

"Get the special spot remover from the laundry room," Donna called from a kneeling position beside her mother. Cecilia leaned back into the overstuffed chair and closed her eyes.

"Elaine Hoffman told me about the crash since her son's a county deputy, but it never occurred to me that it could be our celebs."

She chafed her mother's chilled hands. Donna decided against pointing out that they didn't have any ownership of any celebrities. "It probably isn't. Could be they just blew the whole thing off, or another appointment could have caused a conflict." Besides, what could a singer have done to have the mob after her?

Her mother released a gusty exhale. 'I wish. I'd prefer irresponsibility to injury or death."

"I think we all would."

A sweeping sound carried from the foyer along with a slight snuffling sound. Jasper considered himself part of the cleanup crew.

"Come here, Jasper." Donna made a clicking sound that brought her pup on a run. It also woke Loralee, who bayed in alarm. Jasper joined in, causing her mother to wince. The front bell jingled. The visiting grandparents, the Dickens, wandered in.

"My goodness, are they singing?"

Donna managed a strained smile while signaling to Tennyson. He shepherded the dogs outside. "Ah, I guess you could say that."

Mr. Dickens chuckled. "The outside looks great, and I can see you're doing a great job in here." He glanced at Cecilia, who still had her eyes shut, but her skin had pinked up. "Is she okay?"

Cecilia's eyelids open. "Tired, but that's the holidays." She gave both Mr. and Mrs. Dickens a strained smile. "You know how it is."

Mrs. Dickens pressed her hands together. "It's grand, especially when you can see it through the eyes of a child."

Her husband cupped her elbow and turned her to the stairs. "We need to get some sleep so we can accompany Baby Ethan to church."

His wife readily agreed, and the two of them drifted away. Donna stood to rush after them. "I put some fresh-baked sugar cookies in your snack pantry. Put them in the microwave for twelve seconds if you want them warm."

The two of them thanked her and proceeded up the stairs. When Donna came back into the parlor, Tennyson had brought her mother a snifter of brandy.

Cecilia's shoulders had dropped a little. She took a sip of the potent liquid, then slumped back into the chair. "There's hope for you, Tennyson. I can make you into a gift-giving dynamo." She turned her head to Donna. "Thank goodness you don't buy the cheap liquor."

The incongruity of the comment, considering what may have happened to the visiting celebs, made her giggle. "Yeah, out of all the things you tried to teach me, I settled on buying top-shelf liquor."

Her mother took another sip. "There could have been worse things. I don't remember all those little truisms I threw your way. Some weren't even mine, but came from my mother."

Donna pulled up a white molded plastic chair and sat. Tennyson did likewise and spoke first. "If you knew the name of the singer, I could look it up on social media. If something happened to her, it should be on there."

His idea had merit, but before she could mention her mother couldn't remember the name, her mother did.

"Summer Whispers."

Donna gave her mother a startled glance. Did her mother's memory suddenly shifting into gear or a singer with a stripper's name surprise her more? "I thought you couldn't remember."

"Elaine reminded me."

"Ah, nothing yet." Tennyson scrolled down his phone. "New album release coming soon. There's a mention about her coming to Legacy for the puppies and kitten fundraiser. Someone posted a snide remark about not showing."

"Jerk," Cecilia muttered. "No one would know if people didn't jump on social media and vent. It just makes Legacy look bad. It will be hard to get anybody else to come with the motormouths shouting their discontent."

Donna covered her mother's free hand and squeezed it. "You know what Mark told me when I found that dead stranger in my upstairs parlor?"

"You attract murder?" Her mother lifted her eyebrows.

"No." She leaned away from her mother, but still held her hand. Her mother's smirk let her know it was a joke. "Anyhow, he told me not to worry. Something else would replace it as far as news."

"Hmm." Her mother considered the possibility. "No one ever mentions the dead stranger who had the discourtesy to die in your upstairs parlor?"

"Not any of the guests." Her forced smile felt plastic. Perhaps it wasn't the best example since the guests never lived in the area. "You could invite a local celeb next year."

"Nothing." Tennyson looked up from his phone. "She could be sick and not able to tweet or post."

The doorbell jingled, causing Donna to look at her watch. Nine forty-five and people were still pouring in. Mark Taber peeked into the parlor. "Wow. It looks like a party. I came in the front since the kitchen was dark."

Her mother hoisted her brandy snifter. "Come join us."

Mark grabbed a plastic chair and pulled it close. He gave a long glance to the plate of cookies that Donna passed to him. "The dogs are making a racket outside. You might want to handle that before Madame Litigious, as you dubbed her, tracks the noise to the inn."

Tennyson jumped up and shot out of the room without being asked.

The detective gave a short nod to Cecilia. "I actually came by for you, in a way."

"Why is that?"

Donna would like to know, too. All this time, she fancied Mark either stopped by for the pleasure of her company or food. Right now, the food was winning the competition.

"Well..." He bit into his cookie and chewed for a few seconds, showing better manners than some men. When it looked like he'd take another bite, Donna swiped his cookie. "Hey."

"Talk first. I'll return the cookie. I might even make you coffee."

His shaggy eyebrows went up and down. "I'll talk for coffee. I figure it's okay to tell you since it will be in the paper tomorrow. Summer Whispers and her husband, Slade Woodrift, were in the crash on Route 17 you passed earlier."

Donna placed both hands on her thighs, knowing the news would make her mother go all fluttery.

Cecilia placed the snifter on a small piecrust table. "Oh, my stars. Here I went and had uncharitable thoughts about the woman. What hospital is she at? I should go see her." Her mother pushed herself up and swayed a little.

"Ah, Mom. Why don't you stay the night? I'm sure Loralee wouldn't mind bedding down with Jasper."

She expected her mother to refuse, insisting she was capable of driving. "That sounds good. Is the pink room free?"

Donna curved one arm around her mother's shoulders and guided her to the door. "It is, but we call it the floral room now since I added the floral wing chair and curtains." Donna threw a backward glance over her shoulder, silently asking Mark to stay. He winked, acknowledging her request.

It took a couple of minutes to get her mother settled with a borrowed nightshirt that would probably hang past her knees, her mother joked, as Donna handed her a small bag of emergency toiletries she kept for guests who forgot everything from toothpaste to hairspray.

Her mother sat on the bed with a sigh. "I am tired. Thanks for letting me stay. Maybe I should just keep a bag for such occasions."

Donna didn't answer. As much as she loved her mother, she knew the woman would try to change everything to suit her own personal tastes. "Goodnight, Mother."

"I noticed you don't have the train out yet."

"Not yet." She closed the door, not feeling up to explaining that they weren't even done decorating the house. Her tired feet carried her to the kitchen first where she made some decaf coffee.

Tennyson came in with the dogs swirling around his feet like canine waves. He reached down and scratched each one behind the ears, making her understand why the dogs adored him. "Donna, if you don't mind, I thought I'd take the dogs in my room and watch television with them."

As if that would be a hardship. Good chance the three of them would fall asleep during a holiday special featuring singing cartoon characters or a girl who refused to believe in Santa. "Sounds good to me. Mother is staying the night anyhow. I'll be locking up and shutting down in a few minutes."

Eight individual paws clattered against the linoleum as their owners followed their personal dog whisperer back to his room. The interior kitchen door swung inward a few inches as Mark stuck his head in the narrow opening.

"There you are. I heard voices, but didn't know if guests were raiding your larder."

"Ha. Not anymore. I locked about everything I could lock." She reattached the combination lock to the liquor cabinet. "I'll need to lock the front door, but Santa is still out frolicking. I'm not even sure he's coming back tonight." Her nose wrinkled as she considered what Santa might be doing.

"Is Father Christmas messing with your childhood expectations?" Mark teased as he opened a cabinet and withdrew a heavy white mug.

"Ah, this one messes with my adult expectations. He took Ten out for a beer when a clown rattled his composure."

"A clown?" His hand shot through his hair. "You had a clown here?"

"Nope. A clown doll arrived. Somehow, it was associated with some strange story. You get the clown, you're cursed."

"Yep, saw the movie." Mark moved closer as the coffee maker spat out a thin stream of brown liquid.

"I've put Mother to bed. Tell me the truth about the accident." The man might consider himself sly, but she knew when he withheld information. He was shielding her mother. The woman had a rough day and didn't need anything else.

Mark playfully bumped into her. "Can't fool you." Donna hip checked him, sending him stumbling back a few steps. "Whoa." He held up his hands in surrender. "I'll tell you."

"Go on." She gestured for him to continue.

Mark shoved his cup under the stream and let it fill before replacing the glass pot. "The driver was killed. I have to wonder why."

"Who was driving?"

"Summer Whispers."

An image of a thin woman wearing a gauzy dress walking through a field of wildflowers while singing came to mind. "At least that means she was on her way."

"True. Her husband was the passenger. He was taken to Memorial, but hasn't regained consciousness." Mark pulled out his phone and looked at it. "I should get a call when he comes to."

Shootings were usually personal, except when they weren't. "You think it was her husband?"

"Couldn't be." He added sugar to his coffee and stirred. "Shot came from outside the car. It had the earmarks of a professional."

The only time Herman told her the truth as opposed to a tall tale. This time she wished he'd lied.

Chapter Six

"WHAT EARMARKS?" DONNA'S normally steady voice trembled. Her fear that the sleepy town of Legacy would be taken over by organized crime showed. If it were a possibility, she should know what to watch for.

"Summer was shot in the head with deadly precision while driving a speeding car."

Her attention stuck on the idea that they were speeding. To Legacy or running from danger? "How did you know she was speeding?"

"Skid marks. A pulled emergency brake could have caused the car to spin out about a hundred and eighty degrees. In the end, it hit the guardrail and crumpled the passenger side. The car was traveling over eighty miles per hour. Too fast for the curve, which meant either Summer was speeding to get here or she spotted her killer."

Not crazy fast, but still moving. "How could someone shoot her at that speed?"

"That's what makes me suspicious. It would have to be a two-person effort, a driver and a shooter." He gave an emphatic nod.

"What if it were a rabid fan gone bad, a former lover, a rival, or even a practical joke gone wrong? What if the shooter wasn't even trying to shoot Summer?"

Mark placed his cup on the island top and took a seat on a stool. He stroked his chin. "Why would a fan shoot Summer?"

"Who knows? Plenty of celebs have potshots taken at them. An obsessed fan wrote endless emails, and Ms. Whispers never acknowledged a one."

Mark snorted his opinion, which encouraged Donna to keep going.

"Perhaps the shooter saw one too many movies or played too many first-person shooter video games. They could be mentally ill or could have actually not been aiming for Summer at all."

"Ah, I never considered it could be an accident." His hand stroked his beard stubble.

Herman mentioned his army buddy's great-nephew shooting near the road. "If someone had a high-powered rifle and was shooting at deer near the road, could he have accidentally shot Summer?"

"Could have. A rifle bullet can easily travel a mile. I even heard of a man accidentally shooting his wife. He was over a mile away, shot at a deer, and missed. The bullet penetrated his mobile home and hit his wife while she was pulling a pie out of the oven."

"I imagine she wasn't a happy camper," she remarked as she considered Herman's story. What could she expect when she got something third hand? No doubt, the great-nephew invented the people on the bike to cover his own mistake.

"No. By the time it entered the trailer it had lost speed, but it still caused a flesh wound. I imagine the husband got worse when he arrived home. That's why we have laws about not shooting from the highway, close to one, or across it."

"Laws only work if people follow them." Donna didn't bother to add there wouldn't be any need for the police or even the military if people would naturally do the right thing.

"Yeah, don't I know it." He took another sip of coffee and placed the cup on the counter.

Tired of leaning against the island, Donna perched on a stool. She rested her chin in her cupped hand. If Santa came in late, he could knock. She stayed at the inn when she could. Even though it might be economical to give up her house, she held onto it since it was free and clear. Some people might call her a pessimist, but she preferred practical regarding her actions.

It might be wise to turn off the outside lights to keep anyone from complaining about not being able to sleep at night due to her lights. All she had to do was get a certain detective on his way.

"Ah, Donna." Mark shook his head slowly.

She tried to mentally fill in what he might say. *You're amazing. You're the woman for me. No one can cook as well as you.*

He managed a self-deprecating grin before continuing. "Just when I think I have something sewed up, you have to shoot holes in my theory, causing me to start all over again."

It didn't sound flattering or romantic. "Sorry. I just call them as I see them. There are so many possibilities. Most people aren't hardened killers, but are more likely screw-ups with guns."

"Yeah, right again. I need you on the force."

It wasn't the first time he'd made the remark. "Not sure why. You can drop by, drink my coffee, eat something, and pick my brain for free." The free part stuck in her craw a bit. Here it was almost Christmas. Mark could get her a gift that would give her a clue of what type of relationship or non-relationship they had. If he got her nothing, would she respond like Sharona? Mature women tended to be less excitable. Well, most did.

A phone chime had Mark glancing at his cell. "Slade's awake."

"Do you think that's his real name?"

"Hard to say. Is there any chance the coffee wasn't decaf?"

At the time decaf had seemed like the best choice. The power of suggestion could work miracles. "Seriously, do you think I would serve you decaf?"

"Good deal." He slipped off the stool and headed for the front door. Donna followed with the intention of locking it after he left, which changed when a cab stopped in front of the inn. A large man-shaped silhouette emerged from the car. Staggering up the walk, he spotted them at the door and yelled, "Merry Christmas."

Oh great. An inebriated guest to guide to his room. When Robert arrived, he'd requested the room closest to the rooftop. He'd quipped he wanted to be able to make a fast getaway when the time came. That meant getting him up two flights of stairs.

"Help me get Santa upstairs before you leave."

Mark stared at the sizable man dressed in seasonal regalia and back at Donna. "You need to consider an elevator."

"I've considered it plenty. Money is the issue." It was always the reason behind why she didn't make the changes she wanted. All she could afford at the present was a chair lift, which would cut the stairway in half and ruin its period charm.

Eventually, she would have to get an elevator. The majority of people who stayed at a bed and breakfast were mature individuals who didn't want pools or free breakfasts for their bored children. The rest consisted of women traveling alone or in groups, and couples on romantic weekends. Occasionally, the city landed a conference, and she received some of the overflow guests.

The Columbus re-enactment festival hadn't panned out. Most attendees treated it like a three-day bender. Any place without a bar didn't rate. Truthfully, the idea of drunken guests tumbling down her stairs made her shudder. It wouldn't be as much of a problem with an elevator. It always came back to the item she hadn't put in her original restoration budget.

"Here he comes. Let's get him before he attempts the porch steps." Mark suited his actions to his words, jogged down the stairs, and snagged the arm of the drunk.

"Hey," Robert objected.

The last thing she needed was for him to take a swing at Mark. Donna hustled down the stairs, grabbed his other arm, and patted it with her free hand. "Did you have a nice time in town?"

"Ho, ho, ho." The man stumbled as he laughed, causing Donna and Mark to use their combined muscle to keep him upright. There were times it was good to be a strong female. Although, when was it beneficial to be weak? She considered the alternative while moving her guest up the stairs.

Sure, some women played the dim bulb to get men to rush around and do stuff for them. That only worked so long, and men tended to stop any helpful behavior as a woman aged. There was a time between *babe* and *senior citizen* when an average woman could expect no assistance. The old school gentleman who opened doors and helped with packages was a dying breed. The millennials who replaced them were generally clueless about such behavior, too enthralled with their expensive cell phones to even notice someone needed assistance.

Santa's high-proof breath fanned her face. "You're a good girl."

If that meant she didn't have an active social life and spent most of her waking hours working, then she was. So far, she hadn't reaped any benefits from her behavior. Maybe this was the year. "That I am."

The man stumbled again, causing Mark to pull up hard to keep him from kissing the steps. Donna, caught unaware because of the good girl remark, had dropped Santa's arm. She ducked under

Santa's free arm and pushed up to relieve the weight on Mark.

"Thank the Good Lord." Mark added in a weary voice, "I'm too old to manhandle drunks."

"I'd rather be woman handled," the drunk in question quipped. He turned his bleary eyes on Donna. "Problem with this town is there are too many good girls."

She'd never considered that a problem, but apparently it was for the white-bearded lothario. "That's what I hear." She learned early on in the emergency room that it never mattered what you said to a drunk as long as you kept the tone non-confrontational. She could have just as easily told him another planet joined our solar system since it wouldn't register.

It was also a good time to ask private information since all the shields were down. "Santa, who'd you go see in town?"

The man lurched, forcing her to tighten her grip. Donna could feel Mark's lifted eyebrows without even seeing them. She'd explain if she got any decent info.

"Went to see Trinket and Treasure."

Was he talking about people or a store? Before she could ask, the man continued. "Wanted a good time. It ended up a bummer."

She had a good idea why it was a bummer. Didn't need to go there, but apparently Mark didn't have the same reservations.

"Why was it a bummer?"

Robert stared at his feet as if that might help them work better. As much as Donna figured she'd regret it, she rephrased Mark's initial inquiry. "What was so bad about it?"

"Everything." He grunted. "The girls answered the door all teary-eyed. They heard their favorite folk singer had just died."

"Damn media," Mark grumbled underneath his breath, but not enough to interrupt Robert's explanation.

"They thought it was some big corporation. Same way they stuck a knife," he hiccupped, "into nature's beating heart."

Donna preferred her idiot hunter with a rifle theory. "Why would a corporation kill her?"

Her drunken guest stopped, forcing her and Mark to do likewise. The man gave her an owlish look of disbelief. "Don't you listen?"

Her listening skills were good, although his explanation could use some work. Mark shook his head, probably urging her not to continue her train of questioning. After all, they didn't want to escort an angry Santa up two flights of stairs.

Barking came from deep in the house. She recognized it as Jasper's, and then Loralee's long bay joined it. The canine cacophony grew louder and closer. Tennyson must have opened the door. The dogs came streaming out in full hunt mode.

Robert swayed and moaned. "Make it stop."

Donna wanted the noise to stop too, if only not to wake the Dickens or her mother. "Jasper," she called out, using her authoritative voice. "Stop." He did, but Loralee continued to bay, serving as a canine alarm system.

Her mother appeared on the second-floor landing in her coat and bare feet and snapped her fingers. The basset mix lumbered up the stairs, anxious to get near her beloved owner.

"Mother, don't let the dog..." The guestroom door closed before she could finish her sentence. Her warning not to let the dog on the bed appeared to be a moot point. Tomorrow she'd wash all the bed linen, including the spread.

"Hush." Tennyson followed the dogs' arrival after about a twenty-second interval, which indicated dressing before popping out in the foyer. "Whoa, what happened to Robert?"

The man answered for himself. "Nothing, unfortunately, thanks to that silly granola-eating folk singer."

"Who?" Tennyson glanced at Donna when he asked, but the pretend Santa fielded the answer.

"Autumn Secrets."

Mark cleared his throat. "I think he meant Summer Whispers."

"Oh, yeah, her." Tennyson nodded, aware of the folk singer who never showed for the animal benefit. "Her fans are saying she was taken up on the mother ship. What a waste. She was hot."

"Hot, who's hot?" Robert tried to shake off their hands in order to check out the room, possibly convinced a former cheerleader had snuck by him while he wasn't paying attention.

"No one," Tennyson explained gently as if talking to a four-year-old. "There are no hot women here."

While that was true, it still stung a little. Donna allowed Tennyson to replace her as Robert's right-side support. The three of them moved slowly up the stairs. At least that issue resolved itself. With any luck, everything else would fall into place.

THE ALARM SOUNDED, forcing Donna to look at the vicious entity that always punctured her dreams. This time, she'd been on a cruise. Steel drum music played in the background while she stretched out on a cushy beach lounge chair. A handsome male employee asked her what she wanted.

"I want to keep dreaming."

Before he could answer the alarm went off again, followed by a frantic pounding on her door. Jasper growled but failed to move from his dog bed. It had to be a guest. Odd that they knew which room was hers.

"Donna," Tennyson hissed through the door. "Toilet is overflowing."

"Crap." Her bare feet hit the floor. The cruise ship looked better and better. She belted on her robe as she swung the door open to a disheveled Ten. "Which one?"

"Mine, in the laundry room." After delivering the message, he dashed back toward the laundry room. Jasper, mistaking his action for play, chased after him, barking. Not what people wanted to hear at six in the morning. She definitely didn't need anyone investigating her efforts at plumbing or sanitary containment.

"Jasper! Silence." Her dog threw a confused look over his shoulder, but kept running and barking. When they both reached the laundry room, which had a thin layer of water on the floor, they slid to a stop. Neither Donna nor Jasper had any desire to get their feet wet.

"At least the water stopped running," Tennyson announced from the pocket-sized bathroom.

That was the good news. The bad news included no drain on the first-floor laundry, which meant they would have to mop up everything and disinfect it. "Yeah, great." She pulled up the hem of her bathrobe before wading into the laundry room.

In the corner, near the water heater, stood the broom, mop, and plunger. She made her way to the plunger and grabbed it before entering the bathroom as Tennyson stared at the toilet. The water was at the rim. She shoved the plunger in, splashing water on her robe in the process. *Yuck.*

After a half dozen plunges, the water sucked down to a normal level. Thank goodness. It was the wrong season for tree roots to invade her pipes. Her suspicions rested on too much toilet paper or flushing something down the commode that didn't normally go. "Why didn't you plunge when you saw it was going to overflow?"

The formerly frantic employee blinked, then shook his head. "Plunge?"

Dear, sweet Lord. How could his parents release him into the world without explaining the fundamentals of survival? She'd already taught him laundry and cooking basics. "Okay. Remember the plunger is in the laundry room if this happens again."

"I will."

"Good. I need to start breakfast." She pivoted to leave the room, and Tennyson followed her. Donna turned at the door and gestured to the floor. "You'll have to mop this up first. Then, after emptying out the mop bucket and rinsing it, you'll need to re-mop everything with bleach water."

A heavy sign punctuated her instructions. Donna pretended not to hear. She was already behind schedule as far as breakfast. Today, she had to work at the hospital, too. Even though it had taken her years to get the coveted first shift head nurse position, she'd relinquished it six months ago. As a bed and breakfast owner, she needed to be here for breakfast. The part where she filled other nurses' absences she did not miss. Despite the extra couple of thousand she'd earned for that dubious honor, it wasn't worth the headache.

She turned on the oven as she passed through the kitchen. It would be preheated by the time she returned.

Her switch to second shift went well since no one ever wanted to work second shift. Most wanted first shift to have a semi-normal life where they saw their family and could attend school functions. A few preferred third shift because it allowed them to sleep late. No one ever mentioned liking second shift, but it worked for Donna. She could get breakfast done, rooms made up, and snack pantries filled before she headed out to the hospital.

After that, the guests were on their own. Tennyson was usually there, sometimes Maria, and more recently, her mother. She was the help Donna never asked for, but kept showing up with trumped-up excuses to stop by. After work, Donna would return weary, set up for breakfast, and read any notes that were stuck to the fridge, though Maria tended to text her since it was a more efficient process.

Donna dressed in a hurry, not paying too much attention to her outfit. Instead, her mind was on coffee and the fact she hadn't started any. A quick brush of her teeth completed her preparations. Forget the makeup and jewelry. That was for people who didn't have to deal with overflowing toilets. When she entered the kitchen, her mother was already there.

Cecilia managed to look impeccable, even while wearing the same clothes she had on last night. She sported full makeup, which meant she kept it in her purse. Donna watched while her mother hummed and peered into various unlocked cabinets. "What are you doing?"

Her mother jumped, then slowly turned as she fanned her fingers across her heart. "Land's sake, you scared me sneaking in on cat's paws."

"I wasn't sneaking." Donna was tempted to debate if a person could actually sneak into her own kitchen. "Sorry I frightened you."

"It's all right," her mother answered, while giving her a thorough once-over. Donna cringed because she knew her parent well. "Why don't you run back to the bedroom and put on something more suitable? Some makeup would help, too. You're as white as a ghost."

Her teeth gritted together, Donna mentally seethed. *Remember, she is your mother. You have no clue how much time the two of you have together. Value it.* Her father had taught her the mantra at the tender age of twelve. Too bad he never had a similar one for himself, but she hadn't needed one with him. He never grated on Donna's nerves the way her mother did. The woman always wanted to rearrange everything to her preference, including her children's lives and obviously their appearances as well.

"I'm sorry my appearance offends you."

He mother gave a small chuckle. "There you go. Flying up in the trees again."

"It's hard not to when I haven't been awake ten minutes, and you start in with your makeup remarks. I'm comfortable with who I am. If it upsets you so much, you don't have to look at me."

Her mother stopped her kitchen search to stroke Donna's cheek. "Dear, sweet girl. You're beautiful. I want everyone to know that. Makeup enhances, not covers up. It shows people that you care enough to make an effort. Why do you think I get up every day, put it on, and carefully take if off every night? It's a matter of pride. It's also part of being a Southern woman. Sure, those Northern women may choose not to wear makeup, but that's who they are. It's their heritage."

All her mother needed was Dixie playing softly in the background to make her speech complete. Even though it would be caving, she had a sudden desire to put on lipstick and mascara so as to not betray Southern womanhood. "You start the coffee, and I'll be right back."

While in the bedroom, she changed tops to one that went better with her pants. She also added earrings before slicking her hair back into a low ponytail. "I'm not doing this for my mother," she told her mirror image. *Ha.* The mirror image had a tendency to be a smart aleck.

The scent of coffee greeted her as she opened the door. All good.

She'd poured herself a cup and put the rest in an insulated carafe she'd place on the server with a card that identified it as regular. Her mother was on the phone. Judging by the various *Ohs, No,* and *Oh, reallys,* it was a riveting conversation.

Donna carried the coffee and tea fixings, along with a plate of biscotti, out to the dining room. Her mother was still on the phone when she came back in and started the bacon.

"That was Eloise," her mother informed her. "What can I do to help?"

"You can get the juice, ice water, and milk ready and put it on the server. Normally, Tennyson does it, but he's busy right now." Donna withheld the information of what Ten was doing since it would needlessly embarrass him. "It's odd for Eloise to call so early."

Her mother arranged the filled glass bottles on the tray. A small sniffle erupted as she wiped away a tear with the back of her hand.

"Yes, but I asked her to call as soon as she heard anything else about Summer's accident. Eloise's daughter, Estephany, is a nurse like you. She was on duty when they brought Summer's husband, Slade, in." Her mother spoke while still giving the glass bottles on the tray a second glance.

Eloise would be a direct line to Slade information. Her curiosity piqued, she asked. "What did she say?"

Her mother hoisted up the heavy tray and backed out the door. "I'll tell you in a minute."

"Maybe I should carry the tray." She followed her mother, who refused to relinquish the tray.

"I'm carrying it. That's how people get old. They stop doing things, reasoning they can't do it because they're old. Vicious cycle." Cecilia placed the bottles on the server, frowned at them, and rearranged them, before giving them a final glance.

Donna couldn't take it anymore. She balled her hands on her hips. "What's wrong with the bottles?"

Her mother gave her a surprised look. "Not wrong so much as missing. You need a logo for The Painted Lady Inn. If you had one, it would be on the bottle, your brochures, business cards, you could even have bags printed up with the logo on the front. People could become walking advertisements for the place."

As much as she hated to admit it, her mother had a point. "Good idea, but it sounds like it would cost money."

"It's an investment. Besides, my friend, Meara, has a son who'd do it for you practically free."

"I'm sure that would be news to the son. I'll let you know. I'm more interested in what Eloise had to say about Slade."

"That's a doozy. You won't believe it. The man woke up and has no clue who he is. He forgot everything. Hard to believe, isn't it?"

Donna digested the information as she led the way back to the kitchen. "Traumatic blow to the head can cause short-term memory loss. To forget everything can happen, too, but it seems a little too convenient."

Chapter Seven

TENNYSON SHOWED UP by the time the hash browns were ready to go out. With only a small group, she'd started putting things out family style and letting everyone serve themselves. It would be too big of a hassle and expense to try this with a full inn. So far, it had worked well.

"Did you hear the latest on Summer Whispers' death?" Ten asked, as he lifted the heavy cast iron skillet of smothered hash browns.

"No." Donna wondered if he meant the news about Slade's missing memory. The swinging door flapped back and forth, not providing any type of follow up on the provocative question. She'd have to wait for what was not exactly a meal conversation the guests needed to hear.

She carried a platter of bacon and sausage links. Her mother followed with blueberry pancakes. The scrambled eggs waited in a chafing dish with a small sterno can burning underneath it. Cold eggs never tasted as good as warm ones.

The Dickens were appreciative of the breakfast buffet. A greenish-looking Robert, dressed in jeans and a checked shirt, came down the stairs clutching the banister for dear life. Cecilia took one look at him and clicked her tongue. She waited until the man had reached the dining room before approaching him and whispering in his ear. He nodded and eased into a nearby chair.

Back in the kitchen, Cecilia assembled tomato juice, vanilla, eggs, ginger, coconut water, and a banana near the blender.

Donna suspected she knew what her mother was up to, but she'd ask anyhow. "Is that a hangover cure you're making, per chance?"

"It is." She cracked two eggs into the blender. "It worked wonders with your father."

"I never saw Dad walking around looking like death warmed over."

"No, you wouldn't have. Your father was discreet. There weren't that many times he needed my top-secret recipe, but when he did I carried it to the bedroom."

That explained those odd breakfasts in bed moments, when the breakfast usually came in a glass.

Tennyson picked up the coconut water. Cecilia took it back. "I just started adding coconut water. It helps with dehydration and adds just a hint of coconut."

Donna really wanted to know what tidbit her employee had picked up. She edged closer to Tennyson, who appeared enthralled by the hangover cure. He was probably trying to memorize it for his college friends.

"What did you hear about Summer Whispers?"

The whirl of the blender sounded when Tennyson opened his mouth. She could see his lips moving, but was clueless about what he was saying. Finally, the blender stopped.

"…it sounds weird, but things like this have happened before."

What things? She had no clue. "Could you repeat what you just said? I didn't hear a word of it."

"Me either," her mother added, as she poured the frothy mixture into a tall glass.

The young man shook his head, probably thinking the two of

them were hard of hearing or inattentive. "I *said* word on the street is someone on a rival's street team is the culprit."

Cecilia cocked her head. "Is a street team like a gang? I didn't think we had gangs in Legacy."

"No, we don't *Glam Ma.*" Tennyson used the nickname Cecilia had picked up in a magazine about glamorous grandmas. She'd mentioned once in his hearing that if she had grandchildren, she'd prefer to be called that. Oddly, every time he called her that, she glowed. It was hard to tell if it was the name or the idea of having a grandchild, if only a proxy one. "It's what they call people who promote the artist."

Donna wondered how a public relations person could cause someone's death. That couldn't be in the job description. She could see it in a nine-point font that most people failed to read. *Must be willing to take out rivals of the current client when the need arises.* "Why would a street team do that?"

He gave them both a look of disbelief and inhaled deeply. It made her wonder if she acted the same way when delivering unfamiliar information.

"Okay." Tennyson held up one finger. "A street team is a group of fans. They're crazy about the artist and are willing to work for free."

"That is crazy," Cecilia remarked, as she strolled to the coffee pot with her empty cup.

Tennyson gave the woman a departing glance, probably concerned about her inattentiveness.

"Anyhow," he raised his voice a notch, "the street team gets free stuff like music, swag, T-shirts and stuff. Some take it very seriously. A couple have been obsessed, threatening rivals, spreading rumors online, protesting at concerts, and even fire-bombing a rival's house."

Donna's eyebrows shot up on the last one. She couldn't think of an artist she cared enough about to even know who their competition was. "That's going too far."

"Yeah. That's when they end up kicked off the street team."

Cecilia added, "And arrested." She took a large sip of her coffee.

A thread of a lead materialized in Donna's mind. "Summer Whispers had a street team member like this?"

Tennyson nodded, not elaborating and not helpful.

"Do you know anything about her or him? A name? What has he or she done up to now?" As far-fetched as it sounded it could be a lead. Life and crime seldom followed well-defined pathways.

"Most of the social media chatter favor Kee Kee for being the obsessive one on Summer's team."

"What type of name is that?" She knew every mother wanted her child to be original, but seriously.

Tennyson shrugged. "I doubt it's real when you consider Kee Kee threatened several rivals with everything from face rearrangement to putting sulfuric acid into their soda. Demi Dreams did end up drinking tainted apple juice but couldn't prove it was Kee Kee. She was off tour for two months because of it."

The woman—she assumed it was a woman—sounded off-the-charts crazy. "How could someone get in contact with Kee Kee?"

Her mother put down the cup, placed her hands on the island counter and leaned forward. "Why would you want to get in contact with a psycho?"

Tennyson answered. "Not sure. A lot of the street teams use a chat room app that is Japanese in origin. Everyone has a manga avatar. You could go on and ask about being a member of the street team, but it would seem odd since Summer is dead now."

"Not really." Cecilia chimed in. "Lots of dead singers and actors continue to make money after their death. Often, they're more famous after they die. You could call it a tribute, or a memorial, or something."

It could be done. She could pick out a cute avatar like a dinosaur. She needed a cute name, too. "I could be Cookie Baker."

"Maybe." Tennyson stretched out the word. "It would depend on if it's been taken."

"If it's taken then I could be Chocolate Chip Cookie Baker. How many people could have taken that name?"

"Hard to say. All I know is millions of people are into the chat room thing in Japan. Still, if a street team member did attack, they'd have to be somewhat local if only to track Summer's movements."

Maybe it wasn't a psychotic fan, but she wouldn't know until she looked into it. "I need to get things cleaned up. Can you help me later to set up an account before I go to work?"

"Sure. I'll have to get my work done first because my boss can be a real scrooge."

Her mother laughed much harder than Donna thought the comment deserved. Cecilia even slapped the counter as tears formed in her eyes. "Real Scrooge. Ha-ha. Maybe the Ghost of Christmas past will come visit."

Yeah, like she needed one more thing. "Mother, don't you have a lunch date or something?" She didn't know if her mother had anything planned, but with her busy social schedule, there had to be something for today.

Her mother's laughter cut off in mid-ha as she glanced at her watch. "Oh my, it's already ten. I'm meeting Dollcie at twelve to go over the plans for the Memorial Rose Garden. It's going to be in Centennial Park."

"That sounds important. You better get going," Donna suggested, hoping it would distract her mother enough to get her out of the inn. Mark might call her a loose cannon with her take-charge ways, but Cecilia made her look like an amateur.

"That's good." Her mother pulled a paper towel from a nearby roll and found a marker in the junk drawer. She wrote on the towel. *Rose garden. Lunch with Trevor at one.* "I need to get home and change. I saw Dollcie yesterday, and she'll know good and well I had the same outfit on. I don't want her thinking I'm doing the walk of shame."

Donna didn't want to know how her mother knew that term. When she was a kid, she always thought her mother was clueless about what kids talked about and did. he was convinced her mother knew more than she did. Cecilia Tollhouse might be the senior version of a hipster.

"You go see your friend and have a good time." Did she just say that? Who was the parent? Obviously, Donna needed to get a life. At least that way someone could tell her to go out and have a good time. Maybe her mother would even make her a hangover cure someday. She knew better. As a woman, she'd get a lecture about how it wasn't appropriate for women to be boozing in public. Girls' weekends, along with all-girl vacations, allowed a woman to walk on a slant without any local busybodies to report her actions.

"I will." Her mother gave a finger wave as she left the kitchen.

Tennyson waved back. He waited until Cecilia left the room before adding, "I wish she could be my grandmother."

"Personally, I think she has adopted you since she's given up on having any blood grandchildren."

A huge grin bloomed on Tennyson's face. "I like that idea." He wrapped an arm around Donna and leaned slightly against her.

"That would make you my…"

She could see where this was going and needed to nip it in the bud. She shrugged off the arm and ended the sentence and his assumption. "Your boss. You have a mother, who even now is wondering why you chose to spend the holidays somewhere else."

"You'd be wrong." The grin vanished as Tennyson hunched his shoulders forward. "I don't even have a room anymore. My mother made it into her project room. She boxed up all my stuff and put it in the garage. She even gave away my bed to some family whose house burned down."

"Talk about cold." Even though she had thought it, she shouldn't have said it. It would be the same as rubbing someone's face in the snow after he'd already fallen. Donna cut her eyes to her employee who shuffled to a stool and sat. He propped his drooping head up with his hand. His posture said so much. Guilt about the way she shrugged off his hug pelted her.

Tennyson sighed. He looked straight ahead toward the cabinets as he spoke. "You see why I came back here, and you're not exactly the warm, nurturing type."

Donna crossed her arms, suddenly not regretting her earlier actions as a not so warm and nurturing person.

"All the same," Tennyson tried for an apologetic smile as he explained, "you celebrate the holidays, cook good food, and can be funny when you're not even trying to be."

The fact the resigned young man never even looked at her made her think he was thinking aloud as opposed to talking to her. Still, she knew good and well children often perceived things parents did in a negative light. She tried to consider the parent's viewpoint.

"Do you consider yourself an adult?"

He nodded his head as opposed to answering, but it was enough to show his attentiveness.

"Your parents do, too. They realize you'll graduate and move away. No one wants to go back and live with his or her parents. They'll have curfews, chores, and might even expect you to pay rent."

"Rent!" Tennyson swiveled to face Donna. His eyebrows had disappeared under his bangs. "They'd do that?"

"Parents do it all the time. They're trying to help their children grow up and start their lives, instead of falling back into the way things used to be. It's their way of forcing their children out of the nest."

His brows dropped as he considered the possibility. "Do you think they're making it miserable at home so I will leave?"

"Possibly." Donna wasn't a hundred percent sure this was the message she wanted to deliver. She didn't need angry parents showing up on her doorstep. "Students go to college to prepare for a career, but they learn a great deal more. Often when they return to their home, they think their parents have changed. The student is actually the person who did the changing. Some of these things you might resent about your parents could just be the way you see things now."

Personally, she thought getting rid of the son's bed was on the chilly side. "When you visit, where do you sleep?"

He winced and held up two fingers. "I can sleep on the living room couch, but that involves waiting for my father to quit watching television. Lately, he's been binge watching all these sci-fi shows. I could also use the sleeper sofa in the craft room/office that used to be my room."

The story had just changed. The mother actually did have a bed for her son. "That doesn't sound too bad." Still, she could have saved the bed for her son's first apartment.

"My mom is hot gluing stuff until almost midnight. I never realized they stayed up so late. Cilantro, the cat, considers the sofa bed his. When I use it, he usually tries to sleep on my face or neck. Personally, I think he's trying to suffocate me to keep the sofa bed to himself."

The front door bell jingled. No one should be coming through the front door. The kitchen clock reminded her she had less than an hour before she had to report for her hospital shift.

"Who in tarnation can that be?"

Chapter Eight

A BALDING, MIDDLE-AGED man stood in the foyer flanked by two gangly teenage boys who bore some resemblance to him. The man's gaze inspected the walls. Unaware of Donna's entrance, he peered into the parlor where they'd put up the tree. The boys noticed her and elbowed each other. One put a finger to his lips. It looked as if they hoped to pull one over on dad. It made her wonder if the man would be easy to fool.

The man had his back turned to Donna as he spoke. "This isn't a creepy place like your mother said it would be. I think it's a step above the Traveler's Motor Lodge, which was booked solid."

Her nose wrinkled at the idea that the shabby motel that squatted on the edge of Legacy was booked solid. She assumed people didn't want to visit Legacy in the winter. She also wanted to ask what was supposed to be creepy about the place but knew better. There was a good chance the man might mention the murdered man found in her parlor. As for those other murders, she managed not to have them associated with the inn. She should stop him before he said something else.

The sons laughed and elbowed each other. Donna cleared her throat. "Can I help you?"

The man turned suddenly and shot his sons a telling look that only made them laugh more. The boys had little or no fear of their father. The embarrassed man turned to face her. He blinked. His mouth dropped into a perfect O, making him appear even more comical.

"Did you see a ghost, Dad?"

The man's strange behavior had her curiosity piqued, too. It didn't take a rocket scientist to figure out the man would ask about the rooms, either for right now or in the future. She'd bet he wouldn't want information about the Victorian Christmas tea. Finally, the man spoke.

"Donna Tollhouse, you're the last person I expected to see when I came back to Legacy. I guess you never left."

The comment went right under her skin rather like a fishing hook barb. Why did people who moved away assume they did something better by moving? If no one stayed in Legacy, then it would no longer exist. She surveyed the man from bald spot to lifeless eyes. His uninspired plaid shirt and *dad* jeans strained to contain the body underneath, challenging the fabric. No name came to mind, but the voice sounded somewhat familiar.

"Don't you remember me?" He held out his arms as if to let her get a better look.

Nothing, she had nothing. Maybe he had been ahead of her in school because he certainly looked older than she did. "Do you know my parents?" It might not be a good time to mention her father had died.

"Well, yeah. I know your brother, too." He glanced back at his sons who poked through the travel brochures. One held up a brochure about a zip line and flourished it.

"That's twenty-four miles from here, but it is open in the winter. Many things are closed for the season." Which was another reason Donna assumed guests weren't packing the inn.

"Donna, it's me, your lover boy."

This caused the boys to laugh so hard they held on to each other. Their father turned to the boys and nudged them. He angled his head back in Donna's direction. "Me and Donna were engaged once."

This stopped the boys in mid-chuckle. It sucked the breath out of her lungs, too. The man had to have the weirdest sense of humor ever. The only person she'd ever been engaged to was Thomas. The man bore no resemblance to the handsome jerk who left her family footing the bill for a wedding and reception that never happened.

The man appeared shorter, older, rounder, and generally not that attractive. Age could do that, but memory could also be playing tricks on her. Daniel had suggested her old beau hadn't aged well. The two teen sons gave her the once-over that icked her out. One of them nudged his father with his elbow. "I bet you're sorry now. She's much better looking than Mom."

A tired looking woman in a wrinkled trench coat and a suitcase-sized purse stood in the doorway. She shot an irritated glance at her son and another one at Donna. "I wondered what was taking you so long." The whine in her voice set Donna's nerves on edge, but the tone probably wasn't there before she had married Thomas.

Tennyson slipped out of the kitchen and stood behind Donna. His presence made her stand a little taller. She couldn't care less what Thomas and his brood thought of her, but she wanted to keep his respect.

Thomas nodded at Ten's entrance. "Your son?"

Before she could answer, Tennyson did. "Yes, I am. I'm fortunate to have such a loving, caring mother as Donna." He wrapped one long arm around her shoulders and gave her a hug.

This time she didn't shirk away, realizing his intent. Some people, like Thomas, would think her failure to marry somehow meant she had never gotten over him. That was something she didn't want.

Thomas stared at Tennyson, probably mentally calculating his age so to analyze how quickly she had overcame his departure from her life. He gave a strained smile as he asked, "Do you and your husband run this inn?"

Before Donna could come up with an appropriate answer, Tennyson did for her. "Oh no, my father died in a tragic accident. On his way home from work there was a horrible crash involving a school bus that had burst into flames. My father's natural heroic nature kicked in, and he rescued every child on the bus. Unfortunately, smoke inhalation killed him. The parents were so appreciative they created a park for him."

The bravery of her pretend husband made her tear up—trying not to laugh. It didn't help that Thomas's mouth was hanging open. She managed a slight sniffle. "I know it's been several years," she murmured, "but I still miss him." She managed a small sob. "The inn keeps me busy. My goal is to bring a little joy to other people's lives by providing a nourishing breakfast and a safe place to lay their heads."

The woman glanced at her husband as she pulled a tissue out of her pocket to wipe her eyes. "Thomas, we just have to stay here then."

Tennyson turned slightly away from the family to wrinkle his nose at the pronouncement. Yay, not what she wanted. She had followed Ten's lead with the thought the dysfunctional family would ask some inane question and would be on their way, after Thomas had seen she fared so much better without him. She really had, but now there was the super spouse who had saved children in his last dying moments.

Maria passed through the swinging door with a smile, having

only heard the last comment. "You're in luck. We have room. There was a cancellation at the last moment."

As lies went, it didn't match the one that Tennyson had spun with her aid. The woman put her hands together and looked at Maria hopefully. "Two rooms?"

"We do have two rooms."

Donna tried to catch her sister-in-law's attention, but she was absorbed in the tablet she used for reservations. If Maria would look up once, she'd notice Donna mouthing the words, *no way.*

Her very efficient sister-in-law walked them through the procedures and mentioned the price, which caused Thomas to choke. The man had always been a cheapskate. Too bad it took her so long to realize it.

His wife moved closer and instead of giving him a pat on the back, gave a hard elbow to the ribs. "Stop it. For Pete's sake, I deserve something nice, especially after my mother's funeral."

He grunted, and whatever he was going to say was cut off by the younger son's question. "Do you have video game consoles in the room?"

"No." Donna had never even considered doing so. It would be a high-theft item or would end up being broken.

The other boy leaned forward. "Pay-per-view movies?"

"No." She could see where this was going. Maybe she could discourage them by everything they didn't have. "There's no swimming pool. No hot tub." That should have the family looking somewhere else.

"We do have Wi-Fi, and it's super-fast. You can watch whatever movies you want or play a game online. I'd recommend League of Legends." Tennyson enthusiastically related details about the game to the boys, who nodded now and then and asked a question about procedure and body count.

Morbid little suckers. She was glad not to call them hers. Maria got them settled as Donna gave a wave and retreated to the kitchen. She'd have to head out to work, but the bad news was when she came back to crawl into her bed, her former fiancé would be sleeping right above her. Worse yet, she'd have to fix them all breakfast. Her teeth worried her lip as she considered the possibility.

Normally, she didn't make weekday breakfasts into gourmet-worthy repasts. She just might tomorrow to show Thomas what he'd thrown away. It was petty since she had no interest in the man. Sometimes, a woman had to do what she needed to do if only to feed her ego.

Tennyson entered the kitchen with an apologetic look. He held up his hand before she could even ask him what maggot ate his brain. "I know you're upset with me. I've heard enough about the fiancé who left you at the altar."

Was there anyone Daniel didn't tell? She motioned for Ten to continue.

"Personally, I thought of his appearance as a Ghost of Christmas Past."

Donna pursed her lips and blew out a long breath, trying to maintain her patience. "You do know you have to be dead to be a ghost."

His hand still up, he folded down his thumb and three fingers, only leaving his index finger up. "Call it Christmas Memory Past. This is an opportunity for you to examine the life you didn't have. Bet it doesn't look like such a loss now."

"Couldn't I have experienced this revelation without Thomas and family staying here?"

Tennyson shook his head and dropped his hand. "That one you

can blame on Maria."

"Speaking of Maria, can you bring her up to date on my super heroic late husband and how you're my son? I gotta go." She pulled her purse out of the cabinet. Thank goodness she kept clean scrubs at work. No way would she go back into the hallway and possibly run into the family she least wanted to meet.

She held her hand up in a greeting. "See you later, *son*. You might clue me in later about my husband's name and former career."

He put his hand up to return her goodbye. "David. Brain surgeon."

"No, I don't think so. There's not that many brain surgeons around, and there are none in Legacy. I think he could have a more common job, such as an anesthesiologist. No one ever remembers the person who put them under. David works. Good honest name." She didn't bother to add for a dishonest purpose.

Chapter Nine

O N HER WAY to work, she considered what would happen if her mother or Daniel found out about Thomas booking at the inn. Her brother should be over his teenage outrage, but it would be hard to tell what her mother might do. Yeah, her mom could be a real wild card.

At the red light, her mind hopscotched to what frozen delicacies she had in her freezer. For convenience, she stocked up on items that only had to be baked or warmed up for serving. There were mini-frittatas, French toast casserole, and miniature quiches ready to be stuck in an oven. She could whip up hash brown egg nests along with muesli scones or cinnamon raisin muffins. The scones were less work, but Mark and Tennyson both had a fondness for the muffins.

Her breakfast came together by the time she parked. She jogged up the stairs, unwilling to wait for the elevator while mentally scolding herself for going to so much trouble for a man who threw her over. She decided to shut up her pesky consciousness as she pushed the access door to her floor open. "I'm doing it for me."

A visiting doctor happened to be outside the door. He gave her a short nod, but graciously didn't comment on her talking to herself. For all he knew, she could be talking on a Bluetooth. The first time she saw a person chatting away on a Bluetooth in a department store, she casually edged away from him as did most of the shoppers.

In the locker room, she slipped into her scrub pants while another nurse was getting dressed in street clothes. She recognized the nurse from when she'd worked first shift. "Where are you heading off to in such a rush?"

Marlene shoved her feet into a pair of loafers and swung her purse up on her shoulder. "School play. It's ridiculous they have them in the day. It's something about the teachers not being paid to come back at night."

"Goodness. Some underpaid teachers don't want to spend their evenings at school? Is it worth it?" The question popped out of her mouth before she even realized the thought lurked in her brain, similar to an uninvited guest at a formal reception.

"The play." Marlene wrinkled her nose, "will probably be awful. Most kids will have to be coached through their lines. Last time a kindergartener wet himself."

"Not the play. Marriage, kids, the whole shebang." Donna moved her hand as if directing an orchestra, throwing it up on the last word.

Marlene wrinkled her brow. "Sometimes I wonder. I love my kid. Don't get me wrong. I'm having definite doubts about my slacker husband who spends more time watching sports than he does with his family." She glanced at her watch. "Gotta run. I'll have to sneak in with the play in progress as it is. As long as I'm there to clap my hands for her performance, I'm golden."

"Have fun," Donna encouraged the woman who made the idea of husband and family sound anything but fun.

The slam of the door served as Marlene's answer. Donna pulled her scrub top on and contemplated the road not taken. Hindsight made everything so much clearer. Meeting Thomas today made her realize they had nothing in common. If they had married, she'd be the disappointed spouse. Her children would have a lackluster father who didn't even have the respect of his own children.

Neither Daniel nor she would have ever back talked to their father or deliberately embarrassed him. At one time she'd insisted on wearing a souvenir Native American headdress and that everyone call her Chief Running Deer. Her father had advised her mother—who tried to wrestle the headdress from Donna—to let her wear it. He even went so far as to call her Chief Running Deer. If her behavior embarrassed him, he never mentioned it. He endured it the same way he managed with Daniel getting the lifeguard job when he was fifteen and insisted on wearing the lifeguard shirt everywhere, paired with his aviator sunglasses.

The memory made her grin a little. Her father had been patient with all of them. Maybe Thomas and his clan were not her Christmas Past Memory. It should be all the great Christmases spent with her father. The man loved the holiday and always did it up right with a big, live tree, belting out holiday songs at the top of his lungs, which may have been the result of spiked, homemade eggnog.

Eggnog would be perfect for her Victoria tea. She'd pass on the bourbon in the beverage, at least until all the guests had left. The idea of drinking eggnog alone while listening to her favorite holiday songs caused the tiniest twinge of pity. All the commercials featured happy family members with coordinated outfits. There she went, idealizing the day. Her former fiancé's family holiday would not be movie-worthy, unless it was a horror one. Summer Whispers' husband's seasonal celebration would be a depressing one, if he remembered who he was or what happened.

Shelley, the head shift nurse, looked up from the computer as Donna pushed open the gate to the nurses' station. "I'm glad to see you. Ellen called in sick. So far, I haven't got anyone to take her place."

Donna was scheduled to work, which was why she rushed to arrive. The nurse continued talking, explaining her odd statement.

"Having you here is the equivalent of two regular nurses. Three if they're newbies."

It was good to know she was appreciated somewhere. "Does that mean I get two times the vacation and sick days?"

"Not hardly. I'm not sure the hospital could manage without you. Ellen would have to be gone when they shipped a high-profile patient to our hospital."

In her experience, the more important a patient considered him or herself, the bigger the pain in the backside. "Should I ask who?"

Shelley continued to stare at the computer screen as she searched the schedule for replacement nurses. "Oh, you know that accident that happened out on Route 17 where the singer was shot? Anyhow, the husband who was in the car can't remember anything. They transferred him here when they remembered the visiting doctor is a neurologist who specializes in memory loss."

Donna had almost bumped into the soft-spoken doctor when she'd opened the floor door. The man had caught her talking to herself and said nothing. It could have been that compared to some of his cases, a little self-talk was a minor issue. All she knew about Dr. Whitsel, besides treating the nurses with respect, was he always spoke in a low, comforting voice that would have fit better on a guided meditation CD or in a yoga class. "Why would he be on our floor? Did he have surgery?"

"Most of the other wards are full of pneumonia, flu, and bronchitis sufferers. There were some rooms on the Obstetrics and Gynecology ward, but that would be weird. The same with the children's ward, and Dr. Whitsel didn't want him on the psych ward."

It seemed like the natural place for someone with no memory. "Why not?" Shelley gave her a double take as if she couldn't believe Donna would ask such a thing. Oh yeah, she remembered some of the more colorful patients. "Granny Lowenson still trying to sneak off the unit just wearing a pillowcase over her head?"

"Uh-huh. They also have a new person who thinks he's Napoleon. He's always yelling orders."

"In French?" she asked, not really that interested, but it was the type of statement that needed some type of response. She tapped the keyboard of an idle computer, causing the monitor to flicker to life. Too bad she couldn't remember Summer's husband's last name.

"That's the weird part. Renee who works the floor, whose husband is French, is familiar with the language. She says whatever the man is yelling is not French. The only words she understands are Waterloo, Russia, and Josephine. He upsets the other patients so much they sedated him."

"Hmm, weird." Donna muttered her response halfheartedly as she scrolled down the room roster. There really weren't that many patients on the unit. Most people tried to avoid being laid up during the holidays. Some of them could be trying not to place a black cloud over the holiday season. Too bad Tennyson's grandfather hadn't done likewise. Still, the man couldn't be blamed for his daughter choosing to play the martyr.

"He's in room thirty-two. At the other hospital, those gossipy celebrity magazine reporters were coming up the back stairs to interview the man. One even snapped a photo of him. For his privacy, he's registered under the name Christopher Columbus."

"That name won't raise a few eyebrows? What about the privacy act?" She referred to a government bill requiring a hospital receptionist not to give out the names of patients to anyone. Emotional relatives called demanding to know if their loved one was in their hospital. All Peggy Lee could do was repeat, *I'm not authorized to give out that information.* She complained that it would be better just to have a machine answer the phone.

"Yeah. We all know how well that works. It's a piece of paper that is not enforced. Whoever checked him in had a hard time coming up with a name. Maybe when anyone sees the name, they'll think he's another one, like Napoleon."

"Could be." What she really wanted was to check on the man. Could be he'd remember vital information while she was in the room, the type of random observations most would dismiss as drug-induced hallucinations. A seasoned sleuth like herself could piece things together.

Shelley pushed away from the counter, her rolling chair shooting back about a foot. She nudged Donna in the process. "Go take a look before everyone else arrives. He's a looker, despite being bruised and cut up. Dr. Whitsel wants his memory to return normally. Your *friend,* Detective Tabor, doesn't want anyone feeding him the details. Try not to mention anything."

No one had to tell her twice. She jumped to her feet so fast her stool bounced off Shelley's chair. The woman reached for Donna's tunic. "Wait. Don't say anything to anyone else. None of the other nurses need to know. Some of them can be somewhat star-struck. I only told you since I decided to assign the man to you. Being a mature, experienced nurse, I know you'll remain professional."

"Absolutely," she assured Shelley as she pressed her hand against her scrub pants. She could feel the outline of her phone. With any luck, the man might be asleep, which would allow her to take pictures and analyze his injuries. Mark mentioned the crushed passenger side of the car. It would be hard for the husband to have murdered Summer unless there was a third party.

Of course, if he had, that would ruin her "redneck hunter shooting toward the highway" theory. Her lips firmed into a straight line. *Why did there have to be so many possibilities?* If it were easy, then the case would be solved already. Donna knew from her binge watching of BBC murder mystery shows that when a case looked like it was open and shut, it equaled a frame-up. Even the most dim-witted criminal tried not to leave behind obvious signs such as a cell phone or business card. Sometimes it happened, though.

Whoever killed Summer had left behind a wrecked car, a dead body, and a witness with no memory. She didn't know anything about the bullet since she hadn't talked to Mark. The man tried to withhold information from her, claiming he didn't want it getting out to the public when her lead-time was usually about three to five hours before it appeared in Legacy's only newspaper. Although she had never seen any mention of the type of bullet in the paper, that information could be crucial. It would mean the difference between a hunter's rifle and a Mafia hitman's gun. She wasn't too sure what type of bullets a hitman used, but good chance they'd be the armor-piercing type. A hitman had no time for do-overs. It still didn't explain why a folk singer would be targeted by the criminal element.

Then again, there'd been more than one celebrity whose career received a boost from the Mafia. Her brow wrinkled as she considered the names hooked to the mob. The names evaded her since most of the under the table promotion happened before she'd been born. There'd be no reason for the Family to take out their own rising star. So far, nothing made sense. Maybe it had been a rogue fan from a rival street team. It made as much sense as organized crime.

The door stood open to room thirty-two, as was the hospital

policy. They only closed it when moving, bathing, or doing a procedure. The open door allowed nurses and doctors to glance at the various patients as they strolled down the hall on another errand. It was an easy catch if someone was waving their hands frantically or clutching at their throat because they had lost the handy remote with the call button. Not all people flatlined when they were in distress. The lack of heartbeat always happened afterward.

Donna waited at the door, trying to think of her excuse if caught photographing the injured man. Insurance. Yeah, she'd tell Slade he needed the photos for an insurance claim. It was fairly common to take photos since insurance often denied claims. Pictures were also used to document abuse and assault. Since Slade's wife's death was an open case, she could also label her shutterbug action as forensic evidence.

A raspy voice called out. "I can see your shadow."

A long shadow stretched out on the floor, making Donna look taller and leaner than she currently felt. She might as well go in. Not to enter the room would be strange. "Oh, hello. You're awake?"

The man stared up at her with bloodshot eyes. The bruised right one, along with the swollen bottom lip and the short line of stitches on his chin, made him look like a prizefighter, the losing one. Still, she could see how the high cheekbones and strong chin would appeal to women. His eyebrows were so beautifully arched they had to be professionally shaped.

"I am." He pressed his open hand to his forehead. "I have the mother of all headaches."

"That's to be expected. Let me check your chart before I give you something for it." She strolled to the tablet mounted on the wall that served as their chart. Years ago, they'd made everything digital, when two mistakes occurred because nurses and other doctors were unable to read the attending doctor's handwriting.

Several patients had mistaken the wall tablet for their own use. The fact they couldn't open it without a password or pry it off the wall usually stopped their efforts. She opened the tablet and scrolled through the information. "Good news. You're not on any medications, which means I can get you aspirin. You're not allergic to anything, are you?"

Did she just ask the man who couldn't even remember his name if he knew if he was allergic to anything?

Slade's eyebrows came to a V as he mulled over the question. "I hope not since I don't know."

He tried for a smile but winced instead. The busted lip had to be painful. He might not remember who he was, but he acted like a halfway decent person, not the diva she was expecting. Then again, he wasn't the star.

"Can you tell me what happened?" he asked.

Apparently, no one told him. "What do you know?"

"I was in a car crash, and I lost my memory." His beseeching gaze held Donna's attention.

The man had her feeling sorry for him. Couldn't do that and remain an unbiased crime solver, and Slade could be playing them all. The vital signs made themselves known in beeps and lines. Everything looked good. The heart rate was low.

"You a runner?"

He shrugged.

Did it again. "Never mind. I noticed you had a low heart rate and assumed you were an athlete of some type."

"Wish I knew. I've been awake since they brought me in here. I honestly think they knocked me out for the transport, which I didn't understand."

"Me, either. Let me get you some painkillers. I'll be back in a minute."

She went to the nurses' station where Shelley stood with a phone up to her ear. She gestured to the phone. "No one is answering when they see it's the hospital calling."

"Ah, yeah. I know that feeling from both ends." Donna shook some aspirins out into a paper medicine cup. "I talked to Slade. He told me the other hospital knocked him out before he came here."

Shelley put down her phone, stepped closer to Donna, and whispered, "The guy came in with a bellyful of Vicodin. Luckily, the EMT caught it. We got it in time."

The inference would be Slade had tried to commit suicide by swallowing too many painkillers. Hard to do since hospitals kept everything locked up. The better question would be who gave him the medicine?

Chapter Ten

S OMEONE HAD DRUGGED Slade. She carried the pills to his room, mulling over how the drugs could have entered his system. Who saw him? Obviously, the hospital staff. Who would give him enough Vicodin to overdose? A better question would be why. She doubted the drug procedures were that different at any other hospital. Not only did she sign out every pill she withdrew from the locked drug cabinet, there was also a closed-circuit camera pointed at it.

Inappropriate use would be a career ender. Never mind the part about trying to off some patient. Donna refused to imagine anyone who'd gone into a healing career would kill someone. Sure, there were scary movies that would indicate otherwise, but that was usually fiction.

Before she entered Slade's room, she closed her eyes for a second, trying to emulate her mother's cheerfulness. "I'm back," she uttered in a singsong voice that sounded plastic and just plain creepy.

"Good." He looked up from a The Bible he was thumbing through. He held up the book. "There's nothing to read in here. I even found myself thumbing through this. Nothing about it seems familiar."

She suspected as much, but kept her lips sealed on the subject. She used his blue hospital pitcher and filled his cup before handing it to him. "Here you go. Knock back those pills and you should feel better in no time."

He picked up a pill and stared at it. "It has a B on it."

"That's right. It's for Bayer aspirin. Oddly, the more we find out about drugs and their side effects, the more it keeps us coming back to the humble aspirin as a preferred pain reliever."

"Hmm. Yeah, I guess that makes sense." He put the pill back in the paper cup. "You see, the last time a nurse showed up in her little white uniform and cap and gave me some pills I ended up here. There was some doctor that kept asking me if I felt depressed. He told me I tried to commit suicide."

"Did you?" Once again, she'd opened her mouth and inserted her foot. Slade shrugged his shoulders.

White uniform and hat, she couldn't remember the last time she saw a nurse in that get-up. It had to be more than twenty years ago. The hats were sidelined because they were seldom cleaned and carried infections from room to room. The white dresses were impractical and often so sheer that a slip had to be worn underneath. Then there was the uncomfortable white hose that someone had decided was a must. There was a major celebration when they shifted to scrubs. Only those who didn't work in the hospital expected nurses to wear a white dress and hat. It would be the kind of thing found at a thrift shop or a costume outlet.

"There would have to be a reason for that type of behavior. Right now, I have nothing," He shrugged his shoulders and held up his open hands.

"Tell you what. I'll take the medicine back. You don't have to take it. Your headache is probably more from dehydration. You've got the saline bag rehydrating you. Your headache should be gone in about three to four hours." She picked up the pills, ready to return them to the cabinet. Although, the way her day was going, she might need them.

"No. Wait. What's your name?"

"Donna." She held up the badge that had her name with the designation nurse underneath it. Someone in administration thought using only first names for the staff would make the place a kinder, gentler atmosphere. No one considered there'd be more than one Lisa or Mary in the place. They also didn't recognize that woozy patients would accept nurse, doctor, technician, and aide as a last name.

"My name is..." He held his fingers up to his chest.

"Slade," she finished his sentence before he could. His eyebrows shot up, and his mouth opened slightly before he shut it.

His lips moved slowly shaping the word. "Slade." He blinked and then looked at her. "I think I feel something." He tapped his chest. "My name's Slade."

Was there a camera in the room recording her failure to withhold information? The Spartan room only had a mediocre watercolor not big enough to hide a camera. At least she hoped it wasn't.

"Ah," she hesitated in saying his name as if that could make it worse. Calling him nothing was awkward too. "Let's not mention this to anyone. My mistake. Your memory should come back naturally."

"Why?"

His intense stare made her want to confess the police were hoping he'd reveal vital evidence while his brain suffered the aftereffects of the crash. The fact that a particular detective would be very irate kept her quiet. She wasn't thoroughly convinced Slade hadn't killed his wife or at least arranged it. None of it explained someone dressed in a nurse's disguise pushing drugs on him.

"People want you to remember. All kinds of people."

His eyes narrowed at her answer, probably realizing she was being as vague as possible. People did want him to get his memory back. One of them just happened to be Mark Taber.

She'd turned to leave when he softly called her name. "Donna."

It reminded her of a scene from a horror movie when the woman should have known enough not to turn back but still did, which made her the first victim. Turn back she did, almost certain someone with such a resonant voice and pleasing manner couldn't mean her any harm. "Yes?"

"I'll take those pills now. I can trust you. Everyone else knew my name, but none of them chose to share."

He was laying it on thick now. She couldn't remember what Slade's exact job was, but it must have been a natural born charmer or con man, possibly both. She held out the pills, which he took and swallowed. "You remembered your name on your own?"

He held his thumb up. "Got it. Maybe I have a last name, too?"

"I assume you do. I just don't know it. Wouldn't be Whispers because that's a made-up name if I ever heard one." She fisted her right hand, wanting to smack it against her forehead. "Can't help you there."

She backed out of the room, but not before he said "Whispers" with a puzzled expression. Slade's conversational and motor skills still worked. He was reading when she entered the room, so many of the functional things he learned still applied. Who decided someone had a total memory loss?

She'd attended EMT training. The paramedics were instructed to ask a head injury victim what day it was, their name, and who was the sitting president. It became apparent after a few ambulance runs that not everyone knew the president's name. Sometimes it was safer to ask who won the Super Bowl.

What list of arbitrary questions was Slade asked when he opened his eyes? If it had anything to do with geography, Donna knew she'd fail, head injury or not. A room call light popped on along with a strident beep, one Shelley joked sounded like *Me Now*.

What she needed to do was tell Mark about the fake nurse handing out painkillers. Instead, she trotted to the room with the blinking light. "Can I help you?"

The patient struggled to push herself up in bed. Donna rushed forward. "Let me help." She pushed an extra pillow behind the woman's back. The woman peered at her through bandages.

"What's wrong with my face?" Her fingers tapped the bandages. "Ooh, it feels swollen. Even my lips feel funny."

This was the facelift for Christmas patient. She wasn't sure if the woman's husband gave her a facelift for Christmas or the woman wanted it. Whichever way it was, it was still a pricey present. She covered the woman's hands with her own and pulled her prying fingers away from the bandages.

She held her hands as she spoke. "Right now, your face is swollen, which is a normal reaction. The bandages help conform the shape and lift desired. That's why you have to wear them for now. The good news is the swelling will be gone in time for your holiday pictures."

"Really?" the woman whispered.

"Yes," Donna gave her hands a squeeze, then let go. "Plenty of women had the same operation as you. Two weeks and they were good to go."

"Did they look ten years younger?"

"Yes." Donna hadn't a clue how they looked since she hadn't

seen them before and never saw them later without the bandages. "A few even looked twenty years younger."

"I hope I'm one of the twenty years younger ones."

"I'm sure you will be," Donna assured. She could also be one of those who showed up next year for another body part update. Did no one tell these women that plastic surgery was a continual process that required constant tweaking over the years? "Can I get you anything else?"

"I'm good now. Thank you."

"You're welcome." Ah, this was a sweet one. Her husband didn't deserve her. Most who came in for superficial cosmetic surgery to fight off the rigors of gravity were usually as mean as they come. She assumed the attitude resulted from the pain, the perceived need for surgery, and not being accepted for who they were. They were angry women, but not without reason.

She saw a redheaded nurse at the station. Shelley finally did get someone. That was about as close to a Christmas miracle as she could expect. "Hi, Kathy." She gave the nurse a welcoming smile. "Glad you could make it."

"At this time of year, I can use the money. My feet might not like an extra day, but my kid has his eye on a certain pricey video game."

"You want to get it before the ex does?" She remembered that Kathy and her ex had been into competitive child rearing, always trying to outdo the other.

"Pleeeeease." She lengthened the word into a sneer. "Todd is between jobs and won't even pay a dime in child support. If he shows up with a video game, I'll brain him with it."

"You could sell tickets for that," she joked, knowing the woman would do no such thing.

"Don't tempt me. What's happening on the unit?"

"Not too much with seven of our guests checking out today. We get the good shift when they actually get to go home. First shift promised them the possibility of leaving, but we actually help them pack up."

"It's all good. Anything I need to know?"

"There's a sweetheart in forty who just had a facelift. She could use a confidence booster."

"Got it."

"There's a memory loss in thirty-two. Shelley wanted me to handle it because it's too easy for him to get confused." Normally the nurses shared patients, never claiming one for their own. Although they sometimes divided them up into groups, inevitably someone would get an easy group while the other nurses were run off their feet.

"Oh, him." Kathy made a face. "Shelley told me about him. He remembers enough to cuss and throw things."

Donna almost corrected her until she grasped Shelley's purpose in telling that whopper. The thirty-something nurse would be young enough to recognize Slade. If she didn't know him, she'd remember a handsome man. That gossip alone would have women peeking into the room, and one would be bound to recognize him.

"He's a handful, but I try to comprehend the awfulness of losing everything that made you who you are." That struck the right note.

Kathy looked thoughtful and then wrinkled her nose. "If I could wipe out the years of Todd, I'd be a happier person."

Unfortunately, she was right. Donna had never met the man, but she hated him due to Kathy's stories. It made her wonder if she were bitter about Thomas. Maybe at first, but the man became even less than a memory—more like a shadow in her life.

Shelley swung open the stairway door. "I'm back. Anything

interesting happen while I was gone?" Even though the question was directed at both of them, Donna fielded it.

"Nothing much. I just told Kathy we might lose half our load due to discharges."

Shelley nodded, letting her know her message about Slade was received. "Why don't you bop down to the lounge and get some coffee. They put on a fresh pot. When you get back, Kathy can go.

"Don't have to tell me twice." She race-walked to the door, by-passing the elevator. While on duty, the nurses seldom used the elevators. They were too slow. Doctors also made jokes about how many breaks the nursing staff took while they were clearly on break.

On the stairs, she pulled out her phone. Not too many people would be on the steps since they led to the nurses' lounge and locker room. She dialed Mark's number, but it dropped into voice mail. What could the man be doing when his very valuable witness was here?

She dialed again. Maybe he'd see it was her and pick up. Nothing. Donna glared at her phone, hoping Mark could feel it. Even now, a fake nurse could be escaping across state lines. It would be even worse if the perp were a real nurse. She might as well get the coffee. She'd probably need it after the day she had.

If nothing else, she could text once she got into the lounge. No one was in the lounge, so she retrieved her phone. Personal boundaries could be a tricky thing. She'd caught other nurses leaning over her shoulder when she'd laughed at a text. It was her own fault since she so seldom laughed.

What could she say without telling him she told Slade his name?

Summer's H. is on my ward. Claims he was drugged by a fake nurse. Enough Vicodin to OD. Stomach pump saved him. Sounds suspect 2 me.

The coffee aroma reminded her of her original purpose. She poured coffee into her cup and considered getting one for Kathy, but coffee breaks often served as bathroom and phone breaks. She didn't want to deprive the woman of either.

Her phone burbled. It must be Mark. No, the number was Maria's.

Snack pantries are filled. Going home. Don't feel that good. Ten has everything under control.

Mercy, she hoped so. She didn't want to come in at midnight and find Ten playing online games with the offspring. As horrible scenarios go, that was a mild one. The text alarm sounded again. It was Mark.

Quit doing my job. I'll talk to you later.

Was he joking or criticizing her? It was hard to tell in a text. The detective never used emojis, probably thinking it wasn't manly. Her lips pulled down as she considered how to answer. No answer, that would work. He could think she was busy or mad. Tonight, she'd find out if he was joking. He had better be joking.

The rest of the shift moved as fast as a month of Sundays. The major highlight entered with a hand-delivered survey on if they should have a Secret Santa or not this year.

Kathy sat squarely in the positive camp. "I think it will be fun."

The memory of the tiny plastic pack of tissues Donna got last year made her laugh-cough at the woman's hopefulness. "I bet you've only been in Secret Santa exchanges with women."

"What do you mean? It may have been women only. Why?"

Before Donna could tell her about the Band-Aids, tissues, and an open roll of breath mints she got last year—from a doctor, no less—

Shelley jumped into the conversation.

"Most women are decent gift givers, but not all. About three years ago, Dana from insurance was my Secret Santa. The woman plum forgot she was. I don't know how since she got plenty of stuff from hers. Anyhow, if a male employee draws your name, you're flat out of luck unless his wife jumps in and gets something. Normally, when the guy does remember, they pick something out of their pocket and stick it in your mailbox. Donna, tell her what you got."

"Tissues, bandages, and an open pack of mints."

Kathy's earlier excitement melted way like an ice cube on a summer's day.

Donna continued with a slight sneer in her voice. "My Secret Santa was Dr. Richards. The man bought his wife a sable coat for Christmas."

"That's so politically incorrect." Shelley put both hands on her hips and sniffed.

Donna shook her head, aware the point she wanted to make went astray somewhere. "Anyhow, most people who get your name don't care about you. They're too focused on their own lives and families."

"Yeah, but…"

Kathy looked at both of them, not finishing her sentence. Her shoulders slumped. Another holiday expectation crushed under the heel of reality. It made Donna feel like a joy sucker. Perhaps Kathy should have a Secret Santa even if she didn't sign up for one.

Shelley wadded up the survey and tossed it in the trash. "As much as I hate to say it, no one is going to break the bank to get us gifts. Most of the male doctors are on their third trophy wife, and it takes a great deal of money to keep up the façade. Never mind the alimony and child support for the previous families. The female doctors tend to spend their money on their own families. As for us nurses, the money is usually gone before the check clears the bank. Besides, if you have a little money, wouldn't it be better to do something nice for yourself?"

Normally, Shelley's speech would have been hers. Donna's holiday indulgences included an electric pressure cooker, a high-performance blender, and a professional stand-up mixer. This year she had doubts about splurging on herself. Every year, she rationalized her purchase by reminding herself she had no husband or money to make the grand gesture.

All the chatter about Scrooge and Christmas ghosts made her reconsider the herb garden she was going to buy, complete with grow lights and a hydroponics unit. She should do something different, but she had no clue what it would be.

Chapter Eleven

EVEN THOUGH THEY had a light load on the post-surgery floor, Donna still couldn't leave until her replacement showed or at least enough nurses to run the shift. Shelley let Kathy go first by mutual agreement since she had a kid at home. Babysitters could really eat into a paycheck. If you took advantage of your sitter by not showing up at the stated time, you could be without one. Not speaking from personal experience, but that's what all the nurses with kids said.

Donna wiggled her toes inside her shoes. Her dogs were definitely barking. As soon as she got in the car, she'd remove her shoes. Her shoes had some catchy name like air walk, but no amount of padding made eight plus hours on her feet feel good. She stretched her hands overhead, wondering where the third-shift nurses were. "I'm just glad we're not working twelve-hour shifts anymore."

"Me, too." Shelley agreed with a weary sigh and looked at her watch. "It would be nice if people would show up on time."

"I know it." It usually took an additional fifteen minutes to get the next shift up to speed on what was happening. A conscientious nurse showed up thirty minutes before shift, got changed, and had her coffee when reporting for work. This allowed the previous shift nurse to relay status and actually leave on time. Yeah, Donna used to do that before she bought The Painted Lady Inn. Twenty plus years she'd shown up early, almost never took a sick day, and sometimes worked through her vacation. People with lives often didn't make it on time.

Giselle opened the floor door with a bang. "Oh my goodness, you won't believe what happened. There was some gun battle downtown. All the streets were blocked off. I didn't think I was ever going to get here."

Jayden, their only male nurse, came up behind her. "You, too? I saw the SWAT team and wondered if I'd die before I gave my girlfriend her special surprise. My first thought was I waited too long."

That explained why everyone was about twenty minutes late. As for Jayden's secret surprise, practically every employee at the hospital knew he'd bought an engagement ring. As for waiting too long, his long-standing girlfriend of eight years may have given up hope on taking their relationship to the next level about five years ago. All the same, Donna knew single, working, decent men were hard to come by in Legacy. It would be hard to abandon one because his timetable and yours didn't coincide.

Trudee came in last and offered no explanation. Her sleep-creased face served as reason enough. At last, Donna could go home, while Shelley did a fast update. "What street should I avoid?"

"Pearl, or at least, the part that crosses right through town." Giselle offered the information with a wave.

Jayden turned slightly from Shelley to add, "The part of Main that crosses Pearl is blocked off, too."

"Thanks." Donna waved, anxious to get home, but not so anxious she'd use the stairs. Elevator it was. Late at night when nothing was happening, the lift could be relatively fast. It wouldn't rival any rides at the theme park, but she'd appreciate the break from walking.

In the parking garage, she stared at shadowy, almost deserted place with only a few employee cars left in the shadowy place. Normally, she never thought about the garage. Did they even have a security guard at night? Employees had a card to get in and out, but visitors had to pay and could come and go as they pleased.

Donna stood outside the elevator contemplating her walk across the empty concrete expanse. Twenty years she'd been parking there and never had an issue. No one had, but now with a shootout in town it made her wonder. Legacy might not be as safe as she thought it was. With three solved murders to her name, she should know better.

After each closed case, she reassured herself that someone the victim knew killed them. As an innocent innkeeper/nurse, no one had any reason to kill her, unless they thought she knew something. Did she know anything? There was the fake nurse drugging Slade, but she'd only told Mark. It all boiled down to someone *assuming* she had information.

Would it be better to creep to her car on kitten feet or walk sedately while making noise? In Scouts, her nature hike leader advised the girls to make noise to wake up the snakes who would slither away. She also added the first person wakes the snake up, the second makes him mad, and the third person is bitten. Not too sure how scientifically accurate it was, but it made the girls run to be first while singing loudly.

Undecided, she waited, wondering if Shelley would be down soon. She could wait, but waiting might put a target on her co-worker's back, too. A chill that had nothing to do with the dropping temperatures slid up her back and under her hair. "Okay girl, you got this."

She took a deep breath and strolled in the direction of her car singing, "The itsy-bitsy spider." Sure, she could have sung something more current, but nothing came to mind. Her keys were gripped in her right hand with the jagged key sticking out to be used as a weapon. The instructions from a self-defense class came back to her. *Go for the eyes.*

A loud popping sound sent her screaming across the lot toward her car. She stabbed at the fob, hit the wrong button, and opened her trunk.

"Donna, are you okay?"

Shelley's voice carried even though she remained a silhouette in the dim lighting.

Crap. She prided herself on her professionalism. Running and screaming were not up there with competency. "Ah, after the story about the shootout, I'm a little edgy."

Shelley walked closer, hitting her own keyring fob, making the lights on her SUV flick on. "Understandable, especially since you had that mysterious murder in your inn."

Again with that. Mark had reassured her it would only be a nine-day wonder. Make that a year and several months plus nine days. "Yeah, but do me a favor. Try not to mention it to folks. It's really a great place to stay. I'd even pop for a weekend for you."

"Please, no need to bribe me. I have no special someone to spend a weekend with. I'll take a raincheck." The woman climbed into her SUV and turned over the engine.

No reason to hang around in a drafty parking garage. Probably zero criminal elements hiding in the shadows, but why take a chance? She jumped in her car and locked all the doors before she realized she hadn't checked her backseat.

Donna froze in place, watching the tail lights of Shelly's car vanish around the turn. Hadn't she watched enough news magazine specials to know you always checked the backseat? At one time, she considered buying a pickup so she wouldn't have a back seat to check. Her pent-up breath swelled her belly as she reached up to turn on the interior lights. The killer could lunge forward, putting a gun to her head once he realized his moment of surprise had disappeared.

Lights on. She had to look. Donna cut her head slightly to see the angular brown edges of the back seat. Her breath swooshed out. No killer. Instead, she had her back seat crammed with decorations she'd loaded from her house. She drooped against the seat. "Oh my stars. I'm a gnat on a hot griddle."

Grateful that no one had witnessed her panic, she punched on her radio for a distraction. Some bizarre song about a hippopotamus came on. She always hated that song even as a kid. Logic dictated that no parent would get their child a dangerous wild animal that practically rivaled the elephant as far as size. She never cared for the huge red dog story, either. It couldn't happen. Her father used to tease her, saying she had no sense of whimsy.

Did she have no whimsy? Well, she knew one thing. She wasn't listening to the song anymore, whimsical or not. A dial scan brought her to a golden voice crooner singing about a white Christmas. Not much chance of that happening in Legacy, but at least the song didn't irritate. She backed out and managed to catch up with Shelley as she bumped out of the parking lot.

The radio station she settled on played all holiday songs until December 26. Even though the plan was to keep her mind occupied with the familiar songs, it didn't work. Instead, she hopscotched through scary possible scenarios. The upcoming breakfast that she no longer felt a huge desire to make a big deal out of. She'd still make the muffins for Mark and Tennyson.

Not paying attention, she found herself in the middle of downtown Legacy. It hadn't been her intention to do a drive-by of the shootout area. She still did. Nothing. No police cars, no crime tape, no chalk outlines of bodies on the sidewalk. She wouldn't even know anything had happened if Giselle and Jayden hadn't mentioned it. Nothing about the town square suggested recent gunplay. A few of the doors had some lights turned on inside, and others had outside illumination to discourage burglars. It looked about the same. Legacy was notorious for rolling up the sidewalks by eight. Only restaurants, the mall, and the cinema stayed open later.

After taking a spin around the empty town square, she headed home. By this time, everyone should be in bed, including Tennyson. The fairy lights gleamed on the porch railing. It looked like a postcard of all things festive and cozy. Maria should take a photo and put it on their website.

Apparently, no one shut the lights off. A glance down the street revealed several other houses still glowed with colorful lights. As tired as she was, Donna would not stay up to find out the secret time the neighbors turned their lights off. Her neighbors probably had their lights on timers. The light in the kitchen was on, too. Peculiar. Her headlights caught the dark forms of cars. She wasn't sure, but there may have been one too many. Could be Thomas and his wife drove in two separate cars.

The sound of voices reached her as she pushed open the back door. Mark was here. Her eyebrows shot up. Oh yeah, she didn't reply to his text, which usually worried the man. *Sweet, in a way.*

Tennyson turned on the stool and waved at her. "Hi, Mom."

Mark sipped on his soda, acting unperturbed by the greeting.

"I see you caught Mark up with the sudden shifts in my personal history."

"True and everyone is in their room and accounted for."

"Even Mutt and Jeff."

"Especially them."

Mark lifted his glass up. "I think we should toast Tennyson. He managed to turn aside all requests for liquor, porn, and smokes from the troublesome teens."

"Wow, sounds like a rough night." She patted Ten's shoulder. "Well done, son."

The three of them laughed. The interior door swung open and a robe-and-pajama-clad Thomas stood there. "It sounded like a party so I decided to investigate."

His appearance silenced their mirth faster than a bucket of ice-cold water. Mark reacted first, slipping off his stool, straightening his back, and pushing back his shoulders. His eyes narrowed, and his face folded into lines that caused lawbreakers to expect no leniency. "This is a staff only room. You have a room of your own, along with the use of the parlors and dining room. You even have run of the front porch. There was a reason the door wasn't propped open."

She had to do a double-take. She'd never seen Mark this bristly. Well, not without a criminal in the direct vicinity. She placed her hand on his arm. "Let's not get so riled up. Thomas didn't know." She kept her hand on the detective's arm, feeling like she was holding back a vicious canine.

Come to think of it, where was her dog? A quick look located Jasper sleeping unperturbed in his dog bed, showing no reaction to the intruder. Thank goodness he wasn't quick on the bark, or he'd spend a good part of his day barking at the various strangers walking through his territory. Still, she could feel Mark vibrating underneath her fingers. He certainly wanted to sink his teeth into something or someone.

"Do you need anything?" Donna had equipped the rooms with

everything she could think of, from bathrobes to makeup remover towelettes. She even put a printout of the weather and things to do in the surrounding area on each bedside table.

Thomas stared at Mark, probably some stupid male contest which had to replace squeezing each other's hand. She knew there'd be no handshaking between the two men.

"Can I talk to you privately?" Thomas motioned to the foyer.

Not exactly what she wanted to do at the end of a long, troublesome day full of questions with no answers. Outside of letting Mark take a bite out of him, it seemed like her only alternative. "Okay." Her agreement lacked both energy and enthusiasm. She managed to push out the word, making it sound anything but okay.

Thomas went out into the hall first, and Donna followed. Tennyson and Mark had already started moving toward the door before she did. Yeah, real private.

"All right. What do you have to say?" She placed both hands on her hips, unwilling to be the naïve female Thomas had run roughshod over. It was hard to remember what she thought was so wonderful about him that made her think she had to marry him. Hard to believe she was so gaga about the self-absorbed man. Her father referred to him as all flash, no substance. That was about as close as he came to forbidding the marriage. Most fathers would have been furious after being stuck with several thousands of dollars in lost deposits, but her father told her it was a small price to pay.

Thomas grabbed her right hand, pulling it off her hip. His actions surprised her, but not enough to suffer through them. She snatched back her hand. "Whatever you have to say can be said without touching." She heard a growl behind the kitchen door and wasn't totally sure Jasper had woken up.

"You're right." He didn't bother to take a step back, so Donna did.

Thomas waved his hands in the air, reminiscent of a petty officer landing planes on an aircraft carrier before he finally spoke. "It's you, Donna. Seeing you here makes me realize what an incredible fool I was for leaving you at the altar."

"Amen!" A masculine voice confirmed the stupidity of the long-ago actions.

Thomas's head swung from side to side. "What was that?"

"My phone," Donna lied, not wanting him to guess his apology had more than an audience of one. "I'm really into gospel music. The *amen* is for text messages. When it's an actual call, it plays 'When the Saints Go Marching In.'"

"I'd like to hear it."

"Never mind. You were regretting your decision to take off with someone else. Couldn't you have thought of your reluctance before the non-refundable deposits were made?"

Thomas shrugged. "I wanted to tell you, but you had your heart set on a big showy wedding. If I said anything, it would have upset you."

"Lame." She cocked her head and allowed her eyes to go up and down the man before speaking. "You're right about one thing." She held her index finger up. "I had my heart set on a big showy wedding. All my friends had ceremonies, some with white horses pulling a carriage or at a restored plantation home. I wanted mine to be just as grand. When you get right down to it, I never considered what was really important."

Before she could explain she should have spent more time selecting a groom, Thomas interrupted her. "I guess you weren't exactly heartbroken. You married fast enough. Even now, you're entertaining a man in your kitchen and your husband has only been dead…"

"What I do in my kitchen is my own business. You gave up any right to interfere in my life long ago, except you really did make the best choice for both of us. Sometimes it takes hindsight to realize it."

Jasper appeared in the foyer, courtesy of a human hand, she was sure. The puggle blinked sleepily, but when spotting an unknown man, he erupted into a frenzy of barks and growls. His front feet came off the ground in his exertions. Normally, her aging dog saved his energy to bark at blowing leaves. Someone had woken her pooch, riled him up, and then pushed him out the door.

Thomas turned, opened his mouth, but thought better of saying anything.

She watched his plaid robe and striped pajama legs go up the stairs. An epiphany occurred as she watched the man. She never regretted not marrying Thomas. What caused the empty spot in her heart was her failure to achieve the American dream with a husband, two children, and a home. What she didn't realize then, was not everyone needs the same dream.

Chapter Twelve

G RATEFUL THAT JASPER calmed down as soon as Thomas went up the stairs, her hand flattened against the door as she pushed it open. "All right you two."

Both men sat at the island. Mark flipped through a local magazine while Tennyson had a spiral-bound cookbook held up to his face, pretending to study it. *Please.* "I see you're really throwing yourself into the inn keeping business. You can help make breakfast tomorrow."

The cookbook dropped enough to show his astonished expression. "I don't want to fix breakfast tomorrow."

"Me, either," Donna said, well over a desire to impress her unexpected guests.

"Don't." Mark put down his magazine and folded his arms.

"You forget this is a bed and *breakfast*. People expect more for their money than an almost period-accurate room."

"Tell them there was a kitchen disaster. The stove won't work. Inns, hotels, restaurants have problems all the time. Why not you?"

"I plan better. That's why. Besides, we can't penalize the Dickens and Robert because Thomas is lower than a snake's belly." She liked the new grandparents, and boozy Santa was starting to grow on her.

Mark slipped an arm around her shoulders. "Donna, do you really have no clue the man came downstairs to hit on you?"

"What?" She snapped her head up so fast she bumped Mark's

chin, causing him to mutter something best left unsaid. "That's crazy."

"It's idiotic in my opinion, but that was his plan. Why else would he be prowling around late at night in his PJs after his wife is asleep? We have no clue how long he was at that door when he heard your voice and came barging in. Maybe you noticed he was not exactly a fan of mine."

"Ha. You were the one practically growling." Donna stiffened her fingers and poked Mark in the ribs. "What's up with that?"

The slap of the cookbook dropping on the counter signaled Tennyson's departure. She watched him leave with a furrowed brow. "Just when I think I understand the kid, he goes and does something that makes no sense." Donna stepped away from Mark and into the short jut of a hallway that led to a glorified walk-in closet that served as Ten's room.

A sharp trio of knocks brought a muffled response. "I'm fine. Go back to play fighting. You two might discover something."

Weird. Play fighting? What was he talking about? "See you in the morning." The way things were going, morning would be here before she knew it. As of yet, she had no revised solid plans for breakfast.

Mark had on his jacket when she returned to the kitchen. "Not yet, buster. I have an important question to ask you."

"Anything about a fake nurse drugging patients?"

"No." She pulled open the fridge, grabbed the gallon of milk and a glass from the cabinet. "I already know about that one." She poured herself a tall glass of milk. She held up the carton and gestured to him.

"No, I'm fine. Gotta drive, ya know."

"Two of the nurses were late tonight because there was a

shootout in the town square. Truth or fiction?" She sipped the frosty milk as Mark explained.

He laughed, telling her, "Well, it's a little of both."

Crime didn't usually cause this reaction in the detective. She gestured with her hand for him to continue. "You need to share so I know what's so funny."

He rested one hand on the island. "A passerby went past the copy shop. You know the one that's supposed to be open twenty-four hours?"

"I do." So far, the tale wasn't gut-wrenching funny. "I never saw the need for a place to stay open twenty-four seven. Does someone wake up in the middle of the night and decide they need a thousand full-color copies?"

"That could be part of the problem," Mark agreed, before continuing. "Anyhow, this person looks into the lighted copy shop and sees people with guns. Some of the employees had their hands up."

Nothing was funny about that. Perhaps being law enforcement gave his sense of humor a macabre twist. "Mark Taber, you're laughing about a crime in progress."

"Wait." Mark waved his free hand. "It gets better."

Goodness, when she thought she knew the man, some hidden sadistic trait showed up. Donna was ready to push him out the door, only he hadn't finished the details. "Go on." She tilted her glass upward.

"Then one of the employees who had his hands up fell to the ground."

She choked on her milk. Mark slapped her on the back, but she eased away from him. Did she want anyone guffawing about people's fear and trauma touching her?

"The woman who witnessed it all called 911 and told them a

hostage situation was in progress."

"Makes sense. Did you go?"

"Oh, no, the SWAT team suited up and went out. It may have been their very first appearance besides the county fair."

"What happened then?"

Mark leaned against the counter and took a deep breath. "Nothing."

"What do you mean nothing?" She put down her glass and shook her hands emphatically. "You wind me up with this story about the shooting and hostages and say nothing happened?"

He blew out a long breath and had the nerve to wink at her. "Here's how it went down. SWAT team shows up. They use the bullhorn to tell everyone to evacuate with their hands up. All the employees, including the *shot* one, come out. Turns out the guns were water guns. You're right no one comes by late at night wanting copies. They decided to have a bit of fun. I imagine there might be a major talk with their boss tomorrow."

Her earlier apprehensions about Mark fled. "Now, I feel as awkward as a one-legged man in a tap dance competition. Here I thought you were hee-hawing about an actual crime."

"Come on, Donna. You know me better than that. I would never laugh at crime unless it was something really stupid." He laughed at his own joke. "Speaking of that, what's this nonsense about a fake nurse and Slade overdosing?"

She didn't appreciate the word *nonsense*. If she came up with a clue, it was nonsense. If he had one, then it was a humdinger. "I talked with Slade. He was coherent, charming, and knew what was going on."

"Did he know his name was Slade?"

"He did today." No reason to mention how he knew.

Mark pushed off from the island and directed a *significant* look her way. "This happened after he arrived at your hospital?"

"It could have occurred during transport. No, wait, he was drugged then." It looked like Slade's window of discovery was getting smaller and smaller.

"Did he remember anything else?"

"Yes, he did. When he was in Memorial Hospital, a nurse dressed all in white and wearing a cap brought him some painkillers. One of the nurses mentioned he was full of Vicodin."

"Why is this unusual?"

Donna stepped away from the island and held out her arms. "What am I wearing?"

"Scrubs." His chin stroked his chin. "No one wears those little white nurse uniforms anymore, do they?"

"Nope." She held her finger. "*Unless* it's a sitcom, or an old movie, or you might see one in a costume or thrift shop. Anyone who knows anything about nurses knows the hat went out a couple of decades ago."

Mark gave his chin a couple more strokes. "Someone showing up in a white nurse's uniform could be contrived, at the least. Still, he could have made it all up or imagined it. He was heavily medicated."

"After the..." She made quote marks with her fingers in the air. "...nurse..." She wiggled her fingers again, in ending quote marks. "...visited. She gave him enough drugs to kill him off. A paramedic spotted the signs of possible overdose and saved his life."

"How do you know a regular nurse didn't give him the drugs? He's a good-looking fellow. He asked for drugs. She slips him a couple more." Mark waggled his eyebrows.

Her eyes dropped to her watch. It was almost midnight. Here

she was trying to defend her profession. Donna dropped to a stool and placed her elbow on the island to cradle her head in her hand. "I don't know. Maybe a loss of job and criminal charges might dissuade an actual nurse. It could be there's a closed-circuit camera trained on the locked drug cabinet. Every pill has to be signed out. It's a system to prevent people, nurses or doctors, from casually palming pills. You don't have to believe me, go question the man yourself. I'm done here."

"I didn't say I didn't believe you."

That's what he inferred. "Good night. Lock the door behind you. My morning shift starts earlier than yours."

Mark zipped up his coat and muttered something as he walked out.

Normally, she'd ask what, but not tonight. Too tired to care, she nudged Jasper with her toe to let him know they were moving on to the bedroom. Inside her locked bedroom, she dressed for bed even though she was half-tempted to sleep in her clothes, but she had standards.

"Too old to be working two jobs. I'm also too old to put up with men's garbage."

After washing her face and brushing her teeth, she climbed in between clean sheets. "All I need now is to have some horrible nightmare." She regretted the words as soon as she said them.

THE CAR WAS *speeding down the road with the speakers blaring with a female rocker screaming about her fate. Donna peeked over the driver's shoulder and could see the speed had jumped up to ninety, then dropped to eighty-eight again, only to go right back to ninety. The road stretched out ahead, devoid of traffic and curbs. That*

wouldn't last long. Anxiety clawed at her as the driver swerved, trying to root through her purse with one hand.

"Give the woman a hand," she barked at the passenger who was plugged into an MP3 player. He had his eyes closed and beat out a rhythm on his leg known only to himself. She might have better luck with the driver.

She scooted back behind the driver with the black knit cap on. A blond tail of hair hung over her left shoulder. Donna nearly missed it since it blended into her shirt. Someone, not as close as she was, might even mistake her for a man in her nondescript jacket, knit cap, and sunglasses. The delicate features might, at least, make a person take a second look, which would be hard as fast as she was going.

"Tell you what. I'll get you whatever you need out of your purse if you slow down." No response. Donna squeezed herself between the two seats to grab the leather hobo bag. Her hand missed it the first time. She sucked in her lips, determined to get it this time. Nothing. How could that be? She was sure she had it. Her eyes followed the path of her hand. It was even with the top of the bag strap. Her fingers stretched out to snag the wide strip of leather and passed right through it.

Okay, something was not right with this picture. The ghostly entity was she. No wonder no one responded to her questions. Did this mean she was dead and bopping around in other people's lives while they had no clue she was there? That would explain why ghosts had to resort to moving furniture or changing the television channel for attention.

Whose dream was she in anyhow? No problems with staring since no one knew she was there. She half-leaned over the console to check out sleeping beauty in his reclined seat. The perfect brows and chiseled chin without the stitches belonged to Slade. Shelley was right. The man was a looker. The car's speed started to slow.

The driver threw out the rhetorical question as she eased off the gas. "Are you kidding me?"

The woman slowed down. A high-pitched whine startled Donna, but not as much as the jerk of the car as the emergency brake caught.

The car went from screaming down the highway into a slow balletic spin. The purse she tried so hard to retrieve bounced into the air, scattering its contents. Fear filled Slade's newly opened eyes, but shock crowded it out as he looked toward the driver's side. "Summer."

As much as she didn't want to, Donna looked at the driver's side, too. Summer slumped over the steering wheel. Her right hand still gripped the emergency brake. The question was why had she done that. If someone shot at her from the woods, she wouldn't have had time to react.

She must have seen someone. Donna could have seen the culprit if she hadn't wasted her time admiring how pretty Slade was. Thunk. The car stopped spinning, and a white explosion filled the car. A powder coated everything and a slightly acrid smell irritated her nose. The airbags had gone off.

Donna checked her watch, wanting to see how long it took emergency medical personnel to show up. The hand had only made one sweep of her watch before she realized she wasn't in the backseat of Summer Whispers' car.

No, the slight raspy snore to her left was Jasper. She could just make out the glow of the clock radio. It read 3:11.

The dream, vision, or whatever it was ruled out the possibility of a hunter. Summer had tried to prepare for what happened. She slowed down, which meant she saw someone outside the car. The emergency brake move should have surprised most. It had Donna, but hadn't saved Summer.

If she had looked up, she could have seen the car, possibly the shooter. Maybe Donna would have been shot. Could you die if shot in a dream? Probably not, but she was glad the bullet missed her. Where did it go after hitting Summer? Slade lucked out because he'd decided to nap as opposed to sitting upright.

The bedside light hit her like a punch to the eyeballs as she switched it on. All the same, she needed to write this down. A small notebook and pen were in her nightstand drawer for such a moment. *Number one.* Summer was shot. She glanced at Jasper, who slept on, ignoring his restless owner. She scratched that one out. It wouldn't be a huge revelation since they pulled her from a shot-up car. *Number two.* Summer wasn't shot by a hunter. No, she scratched that one out. Mark was never a fan of the theory, even if she was.

What good was a vision if you learned nothing from it? She shoved her pen and notepad back in the drawer. She fisted her hand and punched her pillow. Too bad she couldn't slap her dream memory around and get some real answers, instead of stuff everyone already knew.

Perhaps it would be better not to have a major breakthrough. Mark would refuse to believe she'd dreamed it. If she told him she had, he'd nod and pat her hand, the way he would a five-year-old.

Donna turned off the light, undecided if she should try to reach out for her most recent dream. Perhaps a dream rerun. Instead, the scenery faded into a snowy hill with her father on top, urging her upward.

"Come on, Donna. You can do it. There's nothing you can't do as long as you believe you can."

Chapter Thirteen

A TENTATIVE TAPPING on the bedroom door jerked Donna up as if electrocuted. It had better not be Thomas. Jasper strolled to the door, wagging his tail, which meant it was someone the dog recognized. Her breath whooshed out as her shoulders slumped. Thank goodness. It was too early to be on the defensive.

"You awake?" Tennyson whispered the question through the door. "I started the coffee and put out the tea stuff. Not sure if I know how to do much else."

"I'm up." A quick glance at her clock showed she'd slept through her alarm. Mark had suggested a kitchen fiasco to get out of cooking. She'd overslept. Not exactly a disaster, but it did put her behind schedule. She dashed to the door and opened it a sliver. "Set the oven to four hundred for me."

If nothing else, she could warm up the quiche, the frittatas, and some banana bread. The Dickens weren't early risers. Her store Santa barely made it down in time for breakfast. He'd be content with toast and bacon. The awkward family had her worried. Would Thomas make any mention of his belated apology?

Although, she couldn't call it that much of an apology. *Sorry I was a jerk. I forgot to break up before I took off with my new chick. Oops, I'm bad. In hindsight, I might have stayed with you.* It sounded even worse in daylight. No way did she want to face Thomas.

All she had to do was get dressed, get to the kitchen, and Tennyson could be her handy go-between. She dressed in the first things she found that were clean and raced down the hall, afraid she might be stopped before she reached her kitchen sanctuary. Mark had already made it known to Thomas that the kitchen was forbidden. With any luck, the lesson had stuck.

The clang of glass bottles signified Tennyson was setting up the juice and ice water for the dining room. She hadn't included milk after both the Dickens and Robert ignored it. Maybe she should put it out for the mouthy teenagers. Her eyes rolled upward. They'd probably insist on a cappuccino or a soda. At one time, she considered a cappuccino machine, but she'd need to charge more to rationalize the purchase. Even now, people thought $160 was highway robbery when the chain hotels usually charged at $100 or more for rough towels, wonky Wi-Fi, and no breakfast.

The backdoor shut the same time Tennyson left for the dining room. Donna held her breath. The very last thing she needed was Daniel showing up a few decades too late to defend her honor, but determined to do exactly that. The sharp tattoo of heels had her breathing once more. No brother going postal on a guest. There really wasn't much else to worry about, though Maria hadn't mentioned coming for such a small crowd. Lately, she had missed more mornings than she actually showed. Donna didn't mind too much because she knew eventuality all the *let's help Donna with the inn* attitude would wear off. It'd lasted longer than she expected.

The lipped cookie sheet with the half-thawed quiche went into the oven. The mini-frittatas she baked in the oversized muffin cups since they tended to spread.

"Where is the scalawag?"

Not Maria. Donna turned slowly to the sight of her mother. Attired in jodhpurs, knee-high boots, and a hacking jacket, she swished a riding crop clutched in her right hand back and forth.

No reason to ask who the scalawag was. The better question was how she knew. Maria hadn't recognized the name and wasn't around when Donna was left standing at the altar. Tennyson strolled into the kitchen and smiled at Cecilia. He asked the obvious question. "What are you wearing?"

"It's my riding outfit. Trenton is going to teach me to jump." She moved around Ten, patting him on the shoulder. "Appreciate the heads-up." He nodded his acknowledgment and watched Cecilia leave the kitchen, on her way to the dining room and a possible stay at the county pokey for assault.

"Goodness sake." Donna darted after her mother, who was already in the dining room conversing with Mrs. Dickens.

"Love your outfit. I used to ride some as a girl. Seeing you all decked out brings back memories."

Cecilia smiled at the compliment and angled her head a bit, saying nothing.

Mrs. Dickens held one hand up to her mouth. "Oh, you asked me about the other guests coming down for breakfast."

Go for the unsuspecting. It's what Donna would have done. They gave out the most information, unaware they had done so. She waited curious too.

"Robert, the man who plays Santa," Georgette Dickens said, leaning forward to sotto voce whisper, "drinks. He is never an early riser. Brings in his own booze."

That was news to Donna. Still, there were no posted rules warning guests not to provide their own spirits. All she could hope for was no rowdy parties or headlong plunges down the staircase. Robert never bothered her about breakfast, generally grateful for whatever he got.

"The family with the teenage sons," her mother prompted, with a tight smile.

Donna recognized the expression as a precursor before Cecilia promised to yank a knot in someone's tail. People had treated her tall, muscular father with caution, not wanting to rile him. If they had offended him in any manner, they needed to watch out for her petite mother instead. Her family line may not have coined the term retribution, but they had raised it to an art form, although her mother took the velvet glove approach, as did most Southern women.

Georgette hesitated, which puzzled Donna, since there weren't that many people at the inn. Her husband, Marlin, came around the corner. She waved him down. "Honey, do you know anything about the couple with the sons?"

"You didn't hear them leaving before the crack of dawn? I'm sure at least one of the boys stood by his bedroom and slammed the door repeatedly." He wrinkled his nose, probably questioning the rudeness of some people.

His wife looked preoccupied as she looked up at her husband. "Of course."

Marlin's report of the boys intentionally slamming doors sounded right. She could see the two of them doing that to irritate their father for forcing them to get up so early.

Thomas sneaking out was par for the course. Never mind that it had saved them both an awkward meeting. The man might have even expected her irate relatives to show up. If he did, he had better instincts than she suspected. Another crisis avoided. She slipped back to the kitchen just in time to check on the entrees. Not done and she had guests in the dining room. Her second go-to selection was the pastries and fruit. Ready fast and usually well received.

Her mother tripped into the room, showing a slight disgruntlement by the slow swish of the crop. The woman had been expecting a confrontation and didn't get one. Cecilia might have been biding her time for years and missed her opportunity by a few hours.

The dull clang of the metal lock against the oak cabinet had Donna whirling around. Her mother rocked forward on her toes to peer into the liquor cabinet. This new adventurous woman her mother had morphed into after the death of her husband surprised Donna. She admired her mother's willingness to embrace new things, but occasionally the new things rattled her. "Liquor before ten?"

"Of course not." She dropped back to her heel and pivoted to face Donna. "Where do you keep the champagne?"

"Downstairs with the wine. Why?"

"Georgette thought mimosas would be a nice touch with breakfast." Her mother strolled to the basement door, which was also locked. She rattled the handle since it was a hasp and padlock as opposed to a combination.

"Where would she have gotten an idea like that?" It seemed out of place for a woman who whispered about Robert's drinking habits.

"I may have mentioned it. I was feeling generous since jerk face had left. I do hope you got his credit card number. You could charge him double since the coward crawled out of here. I doubt he'd dispute it." Cecilia rattled the door handle again.

Donna retrieved the key to the basement from the silverware drawer. "Since you offered mimosas you can make them. Go light on the alcohol. I don't want my new grandparents wrecking on the way to visit their darling grandchild."

"Grandchildren." Her mother managed to make the word into a dreamy exclamation.

127

"Don't start. The reason you don't have grandchildren left early this morning. If you had a look at his kids, you'd be grateful not to have any. Besides, no matter what you say, you enjoy your life of fundraisers, book clubs, dinners out, boating, and golf. You're even horseback riding."

Donna undid the padlock and swung the lock hasp free. "Besides, this unexpected encounter with Thomas made me realize a few things."

Her mother swung the door open and switched on the stair light. "What?"

"I didn't truly want to marry Thomas. I wanted to be married because that's what girls did in my era. When he left, I didn't go right out and marry the next man who asked me."

"Someone else asked you?" Her mother, already on the second step, stuck her head out of the open door. "You never told me."

"It wasn't that important. It was Donald, the son of dad's best friend, Walter. I suspected he asked because he felt sorry for me. I could have said yes if I'd really wanted to get married."

Her mother pursed her lips. "Donald was always a nice boy. He became a mechanical engineer. He did marry. No one as nice as you, though."

"Go on, get that champagne. Quit making up could-have-been scenarios. I've accepted that this is my intended life. I wish you would, too."

Her mother sighed. "My only grandchild has four legs."

"You have Loralee. Don't forget Tennyson."

"True."

Her mother's footsteps descended into the basement, ending the conversation. Donna warmed the pastries and banana bread, which Tennyson delivered. As she scooped up the fruit cup, she considered her life. Maybe she had gotten into the habit of deferring things because she expected someone else to step into her life. Buying the inn was her first major move on her own.

The realization stopped her in mid-scoop. Surely not. She'd taken a few trips with a single travelers group, though the majority of the group were widows with hopes of marrying again. While she'd enjoyed the trips, they weren't necessarily to places she'd been dying to go. She just didn't want to travel on her own. She should take a page out of her mother's book and try something new.

Chapter Fourteen

CECILIA EMERGED WITH a bottle held high. "Found it. It's fortunate your basement is cool."

"It's a basement and it's winter." Not heating the basement worked well since it was underground. It usually stayed in the fifties.

Her mother busied herself assembling ingredients for the mimosas. She hummed under her breath, pleased with her suggestion. "Do you have any more fresh strawberries?"

"In the fridge." She placed some bacon in the still hot oven for Robert. As long as the man had bacon, he was happy. You had to respect someone it took so little to please. With Thomas gone, solving the murder of Summer Whispers would make her holiday merrier. It definitely would give Mark a chance of celebrating.

"Mom, do you know anything about Summer Whispers?"

Her mother concentrated on slicing a plump berry only halfway so it could sit on the rim of the champagne flute. "I did hear she was shot. Husband in the hospital. Claims to know nothing. Personally, I think he's guilty. It's always the spouse in these things."

She'd assumed it was Slade until her dream, which she wouldn't be sharing with anyone. "I don't think so. I heard the bullet went through the driver's window and killed Summer. Slade was in the car while it was speeding down the road. No way he could have fired the gun that killed Summer.

Her mother held one flute up, eyeballing the liquid level. "Did the police even check his hands for powder residue?"

The oven buzzer sounded, telling Donna the quiche and frittatas were warm. It would be a rather eggy meal. "I don't know. What would be the point since the shot came from the outside?"

"Hmm, good point." Her mother eyed the quiche and frittatas. "Too many egg dishes. Egg overkill. I'd just go with the quiche."

Even though that was firming up to be her plan, being told by her parent grated a little. Before she could say anything, her mother giggled before adding further explanation. "That way, we can munch down on your tasty frittatas. Make sure to save some for Daniel since I'm sure he'll be here. I'm surprised he isn't already."

As if on cue, Jasper barked when the back door swung open. Her back door swinging open with regularity didn't bother Donna as much as it would some inn owners. Every local member of her family and Tennyson had a key for when she wasn't there.

Daniel's heavy workbooks had a distinctive clop that announced his entry. He jogged into the room. "Donna, are you okay?" He cut his eyes to his mother. "Hi, Mom."

"I'm fine." She portioned out the quiche and put a generous serving on each plate. Donna gestured in Cecilia's direction. "You can lead with the mimosas. I'll follow. Somehow, I think they'll be more excited to see you."

"Too true, even if they'd never admit it." Her mother picked up the tray and nodded to her son. "Stay put, if you want any break-fast."

Robert stood off to the side in conversation with Marlin, who kept nodding at whatever the topic was. Mrs. Dickens sat at the table with her arms crossed, frowning at the two men who were far enough away to exclude her from the conversation.

Cecilia tilted her head in Donna's direction and whispered,

"Looks like we made it just in time."

Robert's booming laughter filled the room, followed by Marlin's. Even though she guessed Robert had delivered an off-color joke or some other scandalous chitchat, it was hard not to smile when the robust ho-ho-hos sounded. The bearded man had his head thrown back in his amusement, and his cheeks flushed. Perhaps Santa was a slightly naughty old elf. If so, Robert channeled him perfectly.

Her mother called out cheerfully, "Breakfast is here."

Marlin hurried back to the table, while Robert called out, "Is that mimosas? If I knew you were serving mimosas in the morning, I'd have made the effort to get up earlier."

At least Donna now knew how to get Robert down the stairs in a hurry.

Georgette snorted at his remark, but it didn't stop her from picking up her flute and taking a sip. "Oh, this is delicious." She smiled up at Cecilia. "I feel so decadent."

Before her mother could say anything, Robert butted in. "If you're wanting to feel decadent..."

Her mother inserted herself in between Georgette and Robert. She flashed the man her *kill' em with charm* expression that included looking upward at someone with an adoring expression. No issue for her mother, but it never worked for Donna, who at five feet nine—barefoot—had trouble looking up to most people when she had her shoes on.

"Robert, I'd love to make you a mimosa."

Even though she knew exactly what her mother was doing, it still sounded like making a spiked OJ for the stand-in Santa would be the joy of her life.

"Ah, that sounds wonderful. I'd love for you to make me one. Truth is, I have an early morning appearance at Legacy West

Elementary School. Can't have Santa showing up with alcohol on his breath. I suppose one wouldn't hurt, especially if I brush my teeth." He chortled at his own remark.

A boozy Santa would disappoint the children, not to mention the administration who took the brunt of the blame for everything that went wrong during a school day. Georgette gave an approving nod while Marlin chose to speak, causing his wife to look at him in shock as if he'd morphed into a giant cockroach.

Marlin held his hand up as if asking for permission to speak. "In Italy, they leave the jolly old man a bottle of wine and a salami. I assume it's red wine." Georgette threw her husband a censorious look as Donna slid the quiches in front of them.

"Oh, I heard about that." Robert nodded. "In Australia, they leave me sherry and a mince pie. Never really cared for either."

He uttered his trademark laugh and even held onto his belly as he did so. Cecilia pulled out a chair at a nearby table indicating he should sit, which he did, although he wasn't done waxing on obviously one of his favorite subjects.

"The German children are a might stingy. They just write me letters." He gave a sigh as if personally offended by the lack of goodies. "In Denmark, they leave rice pudding, which I like, but it's really for the elves."

Donna had to give the man credit. He certainly did his research. "I'll bring your breakfast in a second," she told him.

"No rush." The man beamed at her, making her forget any earlier issues she had with him not living up to her childhood fantasies. "I'll take a mimosa right now, a double."

The misgivings were back as Donna hurried back to the kitchen to avoid comment. Her mother had already beaten her there and had another champagne flute out. "There will be no double mimosas. It is a fruity, light drink with a sense of playfulness. It's not something a person drinks to get drunk."

Her mother chuckled and sliced another strawberry. "Obviously you missed out on garden parties."

"Possibly." She couldn't think of a single garden party since she didn't grow up associating with the local debutantes. Legacy probably had only at a handful at best.

Daniel cleared his throat, reminding her of his presence. He perched on a stool nursing a cup of OJ. Donna did a double take at his choice of beverage. "Are you okay?"

"Yeah." He took another sip. "My stomach's been a little upset with everything that's been happening. Your personal nightmare showing up and Maria is sick."

Thomas, she'd dismissed long ago, but her petty side enjoyed that the man's life had turned out rather mediocre. Every now and then, she'd speculated her father paid him to vanish.

"Oh, that." Donna gave a slight snort. "What's wrong with Maria? I know she hasn't been feeling too hot the last few days." Guilt needled her. She hadn't even checked up on her sister-in-law. Too busy with work, the inn, and nibbling into the details of Summer Whispers' death. She should have at least tried to contact her. It wouldn't have killed her to make a five-minute phone call.

Her brother's forehead furrowed. "When was Maria sick? Besides today?"

Cluelessness must run in the family. It could have been a female thing Maria didn't want to mention to her husband. Men could be so weird about any mention of cramps, but they'd chuckle about a belch or a fart as if still fifth-grade boys. "She apologized for not coming back the last few days. I told her there was no reason to. Maybe a few days the week before. I really don't remember."

Her failure to recognize her sister-in-law's lingering illness sounded so much worse aloud. Most people would think Daniel's failure to even know his wife was sick would be worse than her transgression, but Donna was a nurse.

Her mother, who had finished preparing the mimosa, demonstrated no distress. In fact, the woman bore a slight smile.

"Hmm, she didn't mention it."

As much as she loved her brother, Donna knew his shortcomings. "You're not good around sick people. It could be the reason."

Her brother rocked back on his heels as if she'd hit him. "What do you mean?"

"Remember when I had to go to the hospital to have my tonsils removed?"

"Yeah, why?"

The man didn't remember, but he was only seven. "You asked me if I died could you have my room."

"Daniel, you didn't!" Cecilia reprimanded her son.

He grinned at Donna. "Ah yes. Now, I remember. Your room had the better view of the neighborhood. People did die all the time in operations. My question was a legitimate one."

The man had missed her point altogether. Before she could explain, her mother did.

"It's the last thing Donna needed to hear before going to the hospital. I'll swing by and see Maria after my riding lesson."

Daniel murmured his appreciation. "Now, about those frittatas?"

Five minutes ago, the man's stomach was too queasy to drink coffee. Although, Donna almost pointed out the acid in the juice he was drinking wouldn't do him any good. "Getting it. Hear anything about Summer Whispers' death?"

First, Donna had to plate a quiche for Robert. She added his beloved bacon to the plate. Since he was down at the same time as the Dickens, she piled another plate high with the crispy meat. Her mother handed her a fruit cup as Daniel spoke.

"I wish the men would stop talking about that. They sound like a gossipy bunch of old…"

Both Donna and Cecilia stopped what they were doing to glare at Daniel.

He sputtered to a stop and then finally added, "…men."

Information could come from the oddest places, such as the phone call from Herman's old war buddy relating the antics of his young redneck relative. Could be one of the construction crew had heard something.

"What are they saying?" Donna asked.

A cheese Danish completed the tray. She tried to give it to her mother to take out, but she waved her off. "I want to hear this."

Like she didn't? She was the one who asked the question. "Daniel, hold the thought. I need to deliver the food."

Her rapid stride could have left a minor wind tunnel in her wake. She placed the dishes on Robert's table and headed for the Dickens' table. Georgette had been scolding her husband for leaving her and talking to Robert. Marlin thanked her as she placed the bacon on the table. His eyes begged her to stop and talk, but she had clues to uncover.

"You're welcome. Enjoy your time with your precious grandchild." Changing the subject was the best she could do.

When she entered the kitchen, Daniel and Cecilia were chatting and chewing. Helping themselves to food didn't bother her as much as possibly missing a vital tidbit. "Did I miss anything?"

"Ketchup. I could use some ketchup." Even though her brother had always put ketchup on anything he ate, with the exception of dessert, it still irked her. Normally, she'd tell him to get it himself since he knew where it was. This time, she got it. She didn't want him to interrupt his conversation.

She grabbed the plastic bottle and carried it over to the island. Donna dangled it over his head with the possible intention of dropping it the tiniest bit, but Daniel reached up and grabbed the bottle, squeezing it. The slightly open lid flew up, releasing a spurt of tomato sauce in her face.

"You did that on purpose!" She complained, while wiping her face clean with a paper towel.

Her brother turned to look at her and laughed. "I don't think I could have if I tried. Serves you right."

Her not-so-secret consideration of bouncing the bottle on his head backfired. She cleaned her face and made herself a plate before sitting down with her family. "What's the news so far?"

Cecilia summarized what had been said previously. "Mari, the master carpenter's wife, is a huge Summer Whispers fan. She's even been out to the site of the accident, leaving flowers."

Donna remembered passing by the scene. "It was up on Route 17. Didn't know who was involved at the time.

Her brother continued to explain the disappearing debris. "The police cleaned up the big stuff, but when I drove by the second time people were milling around picking up glass and putting it into bags. Other people were photographing the site. There was even a shoving match. I had to stop since Alex recognized his wife as one of the shovers."

This was unexpected. Donna had her laden fork almost to her mouth and stopped in mid-action. "What was the deal?"

Daniel shook his head. "Weird. I got out of the truck, because they may have been two skinny women, but they wanted to tear each other's eyes out. We both had to grab a woman and pull them apart. Alex grabbed his wife, of course. Even so, they kept hurling insults at each other. The one I grabbed kept kicking me in the shins."

"Imagine that. You grab a strange woman, and she kicks you."

Her brother glared, but kept talking. "The police showed up. Someone had called them. Luckily, by that time Mari and Hannah had calmed down. Turns out Mari and her friends had come to pick up stuff for a memorial they plan to build for Summer. Hannah and her group were there for pictures of where their current idol's rival died. They're going to post them to social media."

Her mother clicked her tongue in disapproval. "That's morbid."

There was a silence where Donna was supposed to agree. Instead, she tried to remember the name of a possible rival performer. "Do you know who the rival was?"

Daniel shrugged. "Winter's Dirge?"

"You made that up. I can't imagine any singer calling herself that."

"It could happen. Maybe a heavy metal band. They'd scream lyrics about the cold skeletal hand of winter."

Her mother held up a hand, halting the conversational flow. "Gotta run."

"Bye, Mother," Daniel and Donna chorused together.

While her brother's idea about a rival band named Winter's Dirge actually sounded probable, she knew such a group wouldn't have been a rival. Someone would know the actual rival or rivals. While it would be counterintuitive to kill a rival, considering the publicity, plenty of celebrities had killed and, obviously, the public forgot about it. She turned to her mother whose network of friends and associates probably rivaled the FBI and CIA. "Maybe you could find out who Summer's rival is."

Her mother snapped her a two-finger salute. "I will. I helped you solve the last murder. I can do this one, too."

Solve was an overstatement, but if it got her mother nosing around, she'd go with it. "Sounds good."

"How does Mark feel about you messing around in his case?" Daniel asked and munched down on a strip of bacon as he waited for her answer.

Her brother had to go and pour ice water on everything. How did the man feel? Hard to say since they hadn't parted on the best terms last night. "I don't do it for him. I do it for me, but I'm sure he'll appreciate my help."

Her brother blinked as if he hadn't understood her words. Mountain climbers explained their need to scale a mountain by saying, "It's there." A murder mystery had the same allure for her. It wasn't something she could pass by without trying to weave the loose threads into a credible fabric. In truth, she did do it for her. Mark Taber served as her entry into the world of crime-solving. Better yet, the dead man in her uppermost parlor had been her entrance key. Even though she'd found herself wrestling with a killer and staring down the barrel of a gun, she still found it addictive. It could turn out to be a fatal hobby.

Chapter Fifteen

D ONNA DROVE SLOWLY down Route 17, looking for where
Summer met her end. The sedan behind her honked as it sped
around her. No surprise. The normal speed limit was fifty. She'd
only been about ten miles out of Legacy when she came across a
small hill of flowers, teddy bears, and balloons blowing in the wind
on the left shoulder of the road. Fans had cleaned the area of debris,
but there were still skid marks.

She parked on the shoulder and made sure she had her camera
before dashing to the other side. If she took photos, she'd be as
morbid as the other shutterbugs, but her intentions were different.
In the shade of the bordering trees, she looked out at the road and
the skid marks.

The scent of the carnations, lilies, and roses was almost overwhelming as she strolled closer. Laser-printed and colored-marker-
scrawled notes stuck out from the flowers. Rocks held a few to the
gravel shoulder. *Summer, you will be missed. You'll always be in our
hearts. You taught me to hope. I'll never forget you. Summer, you
helped me to be a better person.* Donna squatted as she read each
individual note. Too bad she never had a chance to meet the woman
who inspired such an emotional outpouring. Truly, such a person
couldn't have been the target of a killer.

One white teddy bear with a flowery dress caught her eye. The
soft furry animal with the wide blue eyes had a comforting feel to it.

The folded note attached to it didn't. In strong block letters, the writer had pressed so hard with a black pen that the letters had sunk into the card stock. I WILL AVENGE YOU! Kee Kee. She clutched the bear against her torso. Maybe Summer should have been worried about her fans.

The name sounded familiar, something on the edge of her memory, but the hum of a car engine grew closer, taking her attention. The overgrown tree branches prevented her from seeing the car until it zoomed by. The vehicle went by so fast she only had an impression of a dark SUV with tinted windows. Donna looked the way the car had gone, but the other side of the road bent around the curve, leaving a stand of straggly evergreens blocking the view. If Summer had spotted her would-be killer after she entered the curve there'd been very little to almost no warning.

The wide black skid marks showed the car moving forward. It arced into a turn and into the guardrail where the impromptu memorial stood. Her feet carried her forward to the beginning of the skid. It started right inside the curve. Whoever killed Summer had to have been waiting for her to enter the blind spot before he came charging out. Her hand served as an impromptu sunshade as she stared across the way. No houses, no roads, only a tumble of rocks and wild flowers. Maybe this wasn't the right place. The killer could have been hiding somewhere along the road. Once he saw the car pass, he swung into action.

Outside of that one SUV, no one had passed since she stopped. In such a desolate spot, even now the killer could be watching her. Donna skirted around trees leaning toward the road. No way would she make the mistake of stepping on the road. All it would take was an inattentive driver and she'd be history. On the other side of the curve, similar trees crowded the shoulder, while across the road an aging barn had started to fall in on itself. Sky could be seen through places in the roof. A flat field stretched out beside it. This time of year only weeds grew there. The barn was big enough for a car to hide behind. A skinny, dusty trail cut from behind the field up to the barn.

There would probably be tire prints in the dirt. She could take photos of them. It could be the key to finding the vehicle and its driver. Eager to capture the evidence, Donna got too close to the road. An air horn had her jumping backward as an eighteen-wheeler rumbled by. She watched the truck, thinking it had come out of nowhere. The road obviously had more bends than she'd anticipated.

At her second attempt at crossing, she looked both ways and listened for any hint of wheels on pavement. Nothing. All the same, she ran as if her life depended on it. Once she gained the other side, she ran a few more feet into the rough grass. The last thing she wanted was for her footsteps to destroy evidence. She placed her hands on her knees and examined the trail for possible tire prints. Unfortunately, there were all kinds of marks of recent vehicular traffic. Wide monster tires, regular economy car tires, deep creases from snow tires, and even motorcycle tires. It would be hard to say which one was most recent since they all were mixed. Any distinct treads came when a vehicle had swerved near the edge of the path, leaving a solitary print.

Donna aimed her camera and took a photo. It wasn't noteworthy, but she hadn't risked her life not to take a photo. She walked back toward the barn, hoping somewhere along the way there might be something. It could be anything, from a discarded cigarette or a soda can with DNA.

Even finding possible DNA evidence wouldn't be enough, especially if they couldn't find a match on record. If a deranged fan decided to kill his obsession's rival, he probably wouldn't have DNA on file. His actions, while criminal, didn't necessarily come at the end of a long trail of similar actions. Nope, it could be a one-time thing, which could be either good or bad.

Her eyes swept the ground looking for that one candy wrapper or ammunition case that would seal the deal. Nothing so far. The barn that had looked close from the road had mysteriously moved farther away. The road she'd scampered across had become a ribbon of pavement in the distance. Donna checked her watch. It would be tight to get down to the barn and make it to work on time, especially if the barn kept up its habit of seeming farther and farther away. Should she bother investigating or, better yet, did she have time?

Might as well finish her mission. It would save her a trip back. Her footsteps slowed as she considered what could be waiting behind the barn. What if there were some decaying corpse waiting in the tall grass for her to find? The idea forced her to stop. She shuddered, chafing her arms to rid herself of a sudden chill. "That's too impractical."

The sound of her voice calmed her irrational fear. Crows cawing overhead helped to make the area feel more normal. There wasn't a massacre waiting to be uncovered behind the barn.

She considered the structure as she neared it. A faded logo with a message was on one side. As a child, she enjoyed reading the advertisements aloud as her father navigated down the long county highways. He'd told her the farmers earned money for the slogans and often built barns closer to the road for more revenue. This barn must have been an advertisement-only barn.

She closed one eye trying to figure out the words. "*Chewing Tobacco.*" The chaw stuck in a cheek had fizzled out along with using barns for advertisement. Still, there were a few barns with current ads just as there were some chewing tobacco enthusiasts.

Almost to the barn and no great DNA-gathering opportunities had appeared. She hadn't come prepared. The white bear was still under her arm. Her purse hung from her shoulder. There were no handy evidence-gathering bags inside. Tonight, she'd shove some plastic bags into the purse's outside pocket. Donna unzipped the purse flap and felt around for anything that could serve to preserve evidence. Her fingers slid over smooth plastic. Maybe she did have something after all. Her short nails embedded in the thin plastic and pulled it out. A thin tissue container complete with a few tissues still inside was her prize. If whatever she found wasn't too big, the impromptu bag would serve.

The weeds grew taller around the barn as if aware whoever mowed the fields wouldn't put in any effort on the structure. He'd probably be afraid it might fall on him. The wind blew, causing Donna to regret her choice of fleece vest as an outer garment. While it was practical for short jaunts from the car to the parking garage elevator, she now regretted her choice.

Something falling inside the barn caused a flurry of black wings to lift briefly, visible in the few open spots, before settling back down. It was hard to tell for sure, but Donna was about seventy percent sure those black wings belonged to bats. She tucked the tissue packet underneath the bear so she could run her fingers through her hair. No bugs, thank goodness, and no reason for a bat to swoop down in her hair. There might be evidence in the barn, but this time, she'd defer to the boys in blue.

A look-see behind the barn and she'd head out. The proximity of bats would make the peek a fast one. A swatch of color got her eye. What could it be? Too big for a jacket, too many colors for a tarp, and she was personally glad it wasn't tarp. Usually whatever a tarp covered was often best left hidden.

An urgency to leave welled up in her. Check it out. Be gone. No one in sight, no vehicle, there was a rusted-out plow in some weeds. A quilt with some mouse-chewed holes was her swath of color. It rested on top of a grassy mound or possible moldy hay. A stubby red candle rested near the quilt along with several empty beer bottles. It didn't take a genius to realize this was a local makeout site, a chilly one at this time of year.

Great. She wasted all this time hiking to lovers' lane. No way would she touch anything. The best she could do was suggest the barn as a possible hiding place. Teens riding on pure hormones aside, the barn would work as a hiding place. The murderer could stand by the barn with binoculars. No one would notice anyone, especially in the shadow of the barn.

Donna glanced back at the woods behind the barn. This was probably where the redneck hunter was, although he could have stopped further up. It wouldn't make sense for even the most dimwitted criminal to hide where there was already a vehicle. The murderer would only pick the barn if no one were around.

A fluttering sound along with a high-pitched squeal sent Donna trotting back to her car. She had brought clean scrubs and shoes to put in her locker to take the place of the ones she donned yesterday. Between the dust and the sweat, she'd need to change before reporting for work. If a bat dive-bombed her, then it would be a complete change from the skin out. The only good things about bats, besides eating mosquitoes, was her brother never knew about her fear of the flying rodents. If he had, she could imagine rubber bats attached by thin, almost invisible strings hanging from her ceiling. Little brothers had bizarre senses of humor.

Her breath came as fast as her heartbeats, loud enough to accompany a marching band. By the time she reached the road, she didn't have the energy to shoot across it. Instead, she waited while three trucks lumbered by and a tiny economy car, although she suspected if the last hit her, she'd do more damage to the car than it would to her. With no need to chance it, she waited, and then strolled to the other side.

Once she did, she skirted the clump of evergreens to get nearer to the memorial. If she'd stayed on the other side of the road, she could reach her car with no trouble, but her sense of honor demanded she return the bear. What type of creep stole things from the dead? As she edged into the curve shoulder, she witnessed a dark-haired woman kneeling by the memorial and placing a small box on the ground. Tears poured down her face and caught in her words. "Oh, Summer, if I had only known. There had to be some way I could have helped you."

The woman's grief was so raw and heartbreaking, Donna questioned how well the woman knew the departed. Any inquiry would come off as invasive, but every hour the crime wasn't solved was time for the murderer to flee the area. She moved forward, not sure what to say. Sure, she'd comforted the relatives of many patients, but she never questioned them about a crime at the same time. Common courtesy dictated comfort first, then circle around to what she wanted to know.

The unknown woman's shoulders shook as she sobbed. Perhaps she might know something about Summer's rival. There had to be a tactful way to interrupt her mid-cry to continue her investigation. The bear under her arm started to slip, so she clamped it tighter, which activated a sound box.

"*Hello, friend. It's me, Summer Whispers.*"

146

Donna froze while the crying woman stopped in mid-sob and rocked back on her heels. "It is you. I'm here, listening. What message do you have for me to carry to your fans?"

The woman held her face upward, beaming as if she'd just had a vision. Anything afterward would be a letdown. Donna pulled the bear out from under her arm and pressed on it trying to find the elusive button underneath the synthetic fur that made it talk. Her first three frantic attempts yielded nothing. Her fourth hit a hard plastic box, triggering what she assumed was Summer's voice. *"You're special to me."*

The woman's breath caught. "Do you mean me or all your fans?"

Donna hesitated to push the button again. What if the bear urged her to buy Summer's latest album? The woman held her hands up as if waiting for a divine sign. Perhaps it would be best to retreat to her car. Let the heartbroken fan assume she'd had a special visit from the deceased singer.

Donna backed up slowly. When she got to the edge of the shoulder, a semi whooshing by startled her, causing her to squeeze the chatty bear.

"My most favorite fan is…," the bear revealed in Summer's smooth voice. A high-pitched voice inserted the name. *"Kee Kee."*

The kneeling woman jerked as if someone had stabbed her. "What!" She scrambled to her feet, murmuring something uncomplimentary about Kee Kee before shouting, "She's no true fan!" When she glimpsed Donna, her brows lowered and her body stiffened. "Who are you?"

The tone assured Donna that no information would be forthcoming.

"Just a fan." She backed away, trying not to squeeze the bear. "I'll come back a different time." Donna jogged across the road, unlocked her car, got in, and left without a backward look. With any luck, the distraught fan would assume she'd talked to her idol.

The bear rode next to her in the passenger seat. Donna pushed the bear's tummy, which was the location of the box. *"I'll avenge you!"* The angry voice sounded nothing like Summer's fluttery voice. Kee Kee bore some investigating since the woman at the memorial didn't consider her a true fan. What was a true fan?

Chapter Sixteen

G IGGLING, SOME FEMININE whispering, and an occasional "Oh my God!" filled the air as Donna pushed open the floor access door. The overhead lights that illuminated well but created an unflattering skin tone were the same as always. The strong fruity smell of cleaning solvent drifted on the air. It always managed to defy any detailed description, such as strawberry or citrus. Yep, that was the same.

The nurses' station was empty, but she could hear Shelley's stern voice. "None of you are approved visitors."

This only caused the gaggle of overly made-up preteen females to laugh more and nudge each other. Not even one moved toward the elevator. This was a job for Donna, scary nurse extraordinaire. She straightened her back, making the most of her height and shoes, which was taller than the average twelve-year-old.

"Nurse, are these," she gave the girls a speculative glance, "ruffians bothering my patient and impairing his ability to recover?"

One put up her hand tentatively, while the other four tried to work out if a ruffian was a bad or good thing. One had out her smartphone trying to look up the word but was having issues spelling. "R.U.T.H…"

She gave the girl with her hand up a regal nod.

"We don't want to make Slade sick. We just want him to know we're here for him."

Donna forced herself not to crack a smile. Did their mothers realize they left the house looking like tarts in training? It would be hard to say, but they had to get to the hospital somehow. "Commendable. As devoted as all of you are, the best you can do right now is write your sentiments down."

The five of them stared at her as if she spoke in another language. In fact, she had. The language of terms, expressions, and inferences had faded away into the past. The five of them might not be able to pen a sympathy letter. Having been a young girl once, she figured at least one, or possibly all, were here to interview for the girlfriend position since Summer was now dead. "Pour out your heart to social media. Slade will be able to read your tweets, messages, photos, pins, and everything else. It will help him get better. Make sure he knows who it's from so he can get back to you."

The girls looked at each other, squealed, and stampeded to the elevator. Shelly sidled closer to Donna before whispering, "You do know *your* patient isn't allowed online privileges. They even turned off his cable."

"That's harsh. Staying in the hospital was bad enough, but having nothing to distract you would make it worse."

"Too true." Shelley agreed. "We're also not supposed to let visitors in, male or female. Some women showed up last night. Mona, who was on duty, said their pants were so tight if they had a penny in their pockets, you'd have seen old Abe wincing."

"I'll assume Mona blocked their entry." She didn't even have to see her friend's nod to know the answer. Most nurses didn't enjoy third shift. They liked it less when people messed with the relative quiet of the night.

"You guessed it. Remember that the neurologist, Dr. Whitsel, wants his memory to return naturally."

Female visitors at night. Her first instinct was to dismiss them as overzealous fans. It made her wonder exactly what Slade did to create such a varied fan base. Her athletic shoes made a light squeaking noise as she approached Slade's room for just a peek to see how he was doing. Later on, she'd casually converse with him to see what he did remember.

The man was sitting up in bed and had the hospital robe on backward, revealing a masculine slice of chiseled chest and abs. No way could that be an accident. If the man remembered nothing else, he recalled a peek at a perfectly toned body could get him prime service. A milkshake cup from a popular fast food restaurant sat on his adjustable table. Slade had a book in his lap, turning the pages too fast to be reading.

"Hello." Donna figured she'd already stood at the door too long not to say anything.

Slade swung his head up and smiled. His hand combed back his overlong bangs. "Hello, yourself. I've been waiting for you."

This was a first. A gorgeous younger man smiles at her and announces he'd been waiting for her? *Slow down heart. It's not what it seems.* "Why would you be waiting for me?"

His laugh was low and intimate. "Donna, Donna, don't play coy with me."

The appearance of his late-night visitors was very understandable. She still didn't know what Slade did, but she'd bet he had groupies, though how she was playing coy mystified her. Instead of asking and showing her cluelessness, she slipped into nurse mode. "How are you feeling?"

"After two sponge baths delivered by your very caring associates, I feel clean. If you're asking if I had any memories, I'd have to say no."

"Too bad." It sure would be hard mining him for information. If he were a copper mine, she'd have to nail a *closed* sign over his face. "I feel for you."

She moved around the room straightening the only picture and looking at his hardback book. "*Gone with the Wind*, huh?"

"Portia on first shift went down to the library and got it for me."

The first-shift nurse was always bringing books to patients. If there was a lull in the conversation, Portia used it to explain how the brain gains more neural pathways in reading and loses them while watching television. "That sounds like her. I didn't take you as a historical romance guy."

Slade shrugged. "Dr. Whitsel didn't want me to have a contemporary book. It would tell me too many things he wanted me to discover on my own. I have no clue what I like. It's overwhelming." He dropped his head into his hands.

Donna perched on his bed, attempted to reassure him and solicit information. "Don't be so hard on yourself. You're not the first person to end up in the ward with no memories. Those other people eventually remembered who they were." No need to add it took time, extensive re-teaching, and contact with relatives and friends that accomplished their personal history reclamation. In the end, she could never say if the people actually remembered or said they remembered to please the concerned people hovering around them. Strangely enough, no one had showed up for Slade, if she discounted the pre-teen fans and their adult counterparts.

As difficult as she could be sometimes, she knew her family would show for her if she were ever hospitalized. Her hand hovered above his head. Administrative policy was not to become overly familiar with the patients, which included not getting them special treats. Her eyes drifted to the empty milkshake cup. What major issue would a comforting touch cause? Her fingers landed on his thick, dark hair.

A snort sounded behind her, causing Donna to drop her hand and push off the bed faster than a knife fight in a phone booth.

A familiar gravelly voice commented, "Now I see why I got the bum's rush the other night."

Really, she hadn't kicked him out. She was just tired. Her hand slipped up to rub the back of her neck while her eyes cut to Slade. He'd put his hands down, aware something more interesting might be happening. "We'll talk about it later." She forced the words out through gritted teeth. Mark didn't call her or stop by for twenty-four hours and suddenly she's at fault. As for sitting on Slade's bed and her hand on his hair, she could have been taking his temperature. "Why are you here?"

Mark's hand went to scratch his jaw. "Ah, this is my job. Did you forget?"

"No." She balled her fists on her hips. "This is my job, too."

Slade clapped his hands together. "This is better than television. I take it you two know each other?"

Donna hesitated in answering, unsure if a connection would cause Slade to clam up, but he hadn't exactly given her any info so far.

Mark answered for both of them. "We have a slight acquaintance." He nodded in Donna's direction.

"Slight?" Before she could take total umbrage at being demoted to a slight acquaintanceship, her phone vibrated in her pocket. "I need to get this."

She stepped out of the room, but could still hear Slade talking.

"I may not remember much, but I can tell when a woman is mad. You're in it so deep, you'll need a backhoe to get out." Slade laughed while Mark grumbled.

The corner of Donna's lips tilted up as she considered Mark squirming. She thumbed on her phone. "Hello."

"It's back."

At first, she didn't recognize the panicked voice whispering into her phone. The caller ID showed it was the inn landline. Thomas took his smart-mouth offspring with him, leaving only one person it could be. "Tennyson?"

"Yes, it's me."

"Oh good, just making sure. What's back?" It was too late in the year for cicadas or any other annoying insect hordes.

"The clown."

Oh, good gravy. Was that why he was calling? "Were you in the storage shed?" She thought the clown would stay hidden until the spring or at least until she had time to toss the thing.

"Yes. One of the porch lights went out and I needed the ladder. When I started moving stuff around to get to the ladder, it fell out right at my feet."

Obviously, her hiding abilities were less than crackerjack. "Tennyson, it's my fault."

"No, it's not yours. It's mine. I have never liked clowns, but it didn't excuse my actions." Tennyson's voice became higher and thin, worrying her.

"Leave it. I'll deal with it when I get home." This time, she'd make sure it was gone. No half efforts. She'd drive the offensive doll out to the city dump.

"No, I can't wait." Tennyson's voice sounded stronger, less hysterical. "This is my mission, and I have to accept it."

The boy sounded like he was ready to fly a bombing mission over enemy land. "I'll be home by eleven." It was a long time off since it wasn't even four.

No response. Donna listened, waiting for some acknowledgment until she accepted that Tennyson had truly hung up on her and might be on his way to do something dubious. She hoped it had nothing to do with a fire that could get out of hand.

Mark strolled out of the room and shoved his notebook into his jacket pocket. He gave Donna an odd look. "I got nothing from him. Maybe you should go use your wiles to see if you could do any better."

Sarcasm. She recognized it, but it could qualify as him asking her to help. At least that was what she'd tell him once she managed to pull some quality intel from tall, dark, and clueless.

"Glad to." She held up her index finger. "I need a favor in exchange."

Mark crossed his arms and spread his legs apart. It was his classic *I will not be moved* pose. "I'm not taking Loralee back. You told me your mother was content with the arrangement."

"Hush. Stop getting all prickly. I'm not talking about the dog. I'm worried about Tennyson. He thinks we have a possessed clown at the inn."

Mark rolled his eyes upward. "Only you would have a possessed clown."

Her one hand found purchase on her hip as she narrowed her eyes. "I didn't say the clown was possessed, only that Tennyson thinks it is."

He shifted his jaw slightly and sighed. "I like Tennyson, but he can have some weird ideas."

"You have no clue. The boy has never ever experienced a home-style Christmas."

"What?" Mark dropped his arms and rocked back on his heels.

"Is his family Jewish?"

"Bitter, not Jewish. His mother refuses to celebrate since her father died around or on Christmas. Not sure which. This silly clown doll has him spooked. It arrived via the mail, but no one ordered it. Tennyson wanted to burn it, claiming it was the only way to lift some curse. I just hid it in the shed, and he found it. He sounded all weird on the phone like he was undertaking a kamikaze mission. Could you swing by?"

"All right, but I'm doing this for Tennyson."

"Of course you are. I couldn't expect much from our slight acquaintance."

Slade's robust laugh bounced out into the hallway, making Mark cringe. "I'm really starting to dislike him."

"How could you? He's a victim." She almost elaborated, but stopped when she realized Slade could hear them.

Mark stepped closer to her and lowered his voice. "Could be I dislike him because you like him too well."

The outrageousness of his suggestion made her snort. He almost sounded jealous. Before she could tease him, he held his hand up. "See ya."

"Yeah, see you," she countered. It amazed her that people thought she and Mark had a thing. At one time, she thought they had, but she wasn't so sure anymore. The elevator closed on the detective before she even told him about the bear and Kee Kee's note.

Since she rationalized Mark gave her permission to solicit any info she could from Slade, a plan coalesced, centering on the chatty bear. On her lunch break, she'd retrieve the bear from her car. Then she'd see how much Slade truly remembered.

Chapter Seventeen

S UPPER CONSISTED OF a granola bar washed down with a swig of coffee. Donna consumed that on her way down to the parking garage elevator. A tissue served as her print shield as she detached the note from the bear. What she wanted was for Slade to hear Summer's recorded voice. Maybe she could get the bear to say *I love you* as opposed to the disturbing *I will avenge you.* It sounded like something from a B horror movie.

"What a cute bear. Did you get it from the gift shop?" a visitor asked.

"No, but they do have bears in the gift shop." She lengthened her stride to get away from the inquisitive woman. She might even ask to hold the animal.

Thelma from phlebotomy spotted her. *Great. Ignoring her would mean a delay on any blood sample info.* "Hey, Thelma."

She made a lunge for the elevator, although she normally avoided them.

Thelma yelled after her, "Who's the bear for?" just as the elevator doors closed.

Why hadn't she shoved it in a bag? She peeled off the sweater she normally wore in the building and draped it over the bear. It did make her arm resemble something that might be seen on one of those Internet sites that advertised people too bizarre to be real but are. The elevators all had clocks to let the employees know just how much time they had left on their break. Eight minutes to dash into Slade's room, squeeze the bear, and have the man say something useful.

When the door opened, she sprung out before anyone else, leaving the rest of the occupants grumbling. If they'd been in a hurry, then they'd have jumped out first. Donna glanced furtively both ways. A dietary aide was pushing a loaded cart away from her, but other than that no one was around to see her.

She slid into Slade's room as he used a fork to push a breaded patty around on his plate. Someone in dietary gave the food entrees ambiguous names such as *cowboy patty*, which was today's special. Most would assume it was beef, but she wouldn't bet on it. "How's your dinner?"

"Suspicious." He put down his fork and smiled up at her.

"What?" She didn't quite understand the comment.

"They tell me its food, but I'm suspicious. It makes me wonder what I used to eat."

Good question. Donna almost babbled that Summer was into locally sourced food and was a vegan, but that was her public façade. The woman could have been chucking down cheeseburgers and craft beers in private. "I noticed you had a shake last night."

"Yeah, I did. Vanilla. Kathy called it comfort food. Whatever this is, it's not comfort food." He pushed the tray away.

Kathy would probably show up with a serving of homemade macaroni and cheese with toasted breadcrumbs on top. The fact the divorced forty-something nurse brought Slade goodies surprised her. Donna would have sworn the woman hated men. Just goes to show people will surprise you.

She whipped her sweater off the bear and shifted closer to the bed. Maria had made a similar bear for Daniel when they were dating. Whatever provocative comments her sister-in-law recorded, Donna never heard since her brother ripped the bear out of her hands at the possibility of her squeezing it to make it talk. "Look at this cute little bear I found." She pushed the stomach, expecting to hear Summer's voice possibly recorded off a television or radio interview. Instead, she heard a discordant feminine voice growl. *"Kee Kee is the real star."*

Slade gave the bear a puzzled look, which must have mirrored hers. "Kee Kee is an odd name. Do I know anyone named Kee Kee?" His eyes rolled upward.

She didn't know. It wasn't the message she wanted Slade to hear.

"Kee Kee," he repeated the name again. "It sounds so familiar. I know I had to have heard it before."

Donna stared at Slade as he mused on the name. A couple of times he opened his mouth to speak, then closed his lips. Finally, he shook his head. "Kee Kee was supposed to be Summer's number one fan." His eyes opened more as he pressed a hand to his chest. "I just remembered."

A shrill alarm indicated another patient was in distress. Donna rushed out of the room, leaving the bear behind. The light outside door fourteen blinked off and on. Shelley and Robin pushed the crash cart in that direction. Donna sprinted ahead to prepare the patient. No one ever warned nursing students that the job could be a workout for the legs, heart, and nerves.

Ten minutes later, the doctor on call arrived. The three nurses managed to revive the failing patient and stabilized him. It wasn't anything like the medical television shows where the earnest but incredibly handsome doctor saves the patient. Yeah, those shows had a good half dozen people running to a room. Most hospitals wished they could afford a staff that large.

A phone call home brought the revived man's wife to sit by his bed. Although no one would say it aloud, relatives often had been used as unpaid support staff. Other times they were pains in the rear.

After the adrenaline rush of snatching someone back from death, her energy level did a nosedive, leaving her to shuffle down the hallway in time to hear. *"You're special to me."*

Oh mercy, she'd left the bear in Slade's room. The sound of sobbing reached her. Inside the room, she found Slade hugging the bear, triggering the voice box mechanism, and crying. "She's gone. Summer's gone."

"Yes, she is." It was hard to know what else to say. It seemed too soon to inquire about the shooting. Something everyone else had known about for the last two days was new to Slade. Celebrity news sites that had trumpeted her passing had moved on to the fresher, more scandalous tidbits.

The tears that streamed down his face were real. No faking his personal agony. In the end, why would he bother to fake anything for her? If he were guilty, she could understand the police or a press conference, but not crying his heart out for a second shift nurse. He'd started crying even before she showed up. The bear's fur was damp and matted.

Mark would comment that she didn't think he was guilty because he was so handsome. While it was true attractive people got away with more crimes, she knew Slade wasn't guilty. He had been asleep when everything happened. She'd seen it and, dream or no dream, she believed it.

Kee Kee sounded more and more like a suspect in her opinion. "Do you remember what Kee Kee looks like?"

"Black hair, slender, intense eyes." He spoke into the bear, muffling his words.

It could have easily been the girl crying at the memorial. Donna had stood mere feet from her. Black hair was the most dominant hair color in the world. Some people dyed their hair black, too. Slade's description could fit hundreds of people. It was time to call Mark. He had the manpower and technology she didn't. It didn't mean she was giving up. Her role would be covert.

The detective showed up immediately, which made Donna suspect he was hanging out in the lobby. Either the man had absolutely nothing to do or he had a greater belief in her ability to break through to Slade than she did. He gave her a wink as he breezed past her. "I knew you could do it."

"Do what?" Shelley inquired, looking up from typing in patient notes.

Donna shrugged. "I wish I knew." No one would consider bringing in the bear, which resulted in a traumatic breakdown, as a good thing. Well, no one except Mark. She hadn't expected everything to come at once like a dam bursting. Instead, she'd expected a trickle. A memory of Summer and Slade enjoying a picnic somewhere. Maybe he might remember the two of them singing together. Everything at once was too much for him. The doctor had already given Slade a sedative. The man would be out before third shift arrived with the yummy comfort food.

Donna puttered around the station waiting for Mark to exit. Shelley looked up at her and smiled. "There's not much going on. You could walk your sweetie out to the car when he's ready."

"He's not my sweetie," she protested at the same time Mark stepped into the hallway. He lifted his bushy eyebrows, letting her know he'd heard. What did the man expect from such a slight acquaintanceship? All the same, she didn't give up her chance to walk him out.

She nodded at Shelley. "I'll be back in a little bit."

The head nurse waved her hand in a stop motion. "No rush. It takes time to build a relationship."

As much as Donna wanted to reply, she didn't want Mark to get away. "Hold that thought."

She sprinted for the elevator, which the good detective held for her. They were the only people.

"You wanted to see me?"

"Obviously." She wrinkled her nose at her inane remark. "How's Tennyson?"

"Better. Turns out when he was ten, he destroyed a cousin's clown doll. It bore a remarkable resemblance to the clown that arrived with the train. His not-so-nice cousin was teasing him about his mother not celebrating Christmas. She called his mother weird, and that was all it took. I imagine she wasn't the first one to make a similar comment. After he'd ripped the arms and head off the doll, his loving cousin told him the doll was from some story. When it showed up at his house, he'd be cursed. The only way he could get rid of the curse was by burning it. Of course, he'd forgotten about it until the clown showed up, which triggered his anxiety."

"The clown?" She expected it to be a smoking pile of black ash.

"It's in the back of my car. It's a new doll, and I'm going to drop it off at the shelter where there is bound to be a kid who'll love it."

Mark always did the thoughtful thing. She didn't have the heart to tell him no kid would love that doll. "That's nice." Now, she needed to ease into the other topic. "Get any leads on your case?"

He held up his wrist and looked at his watch. "You held out much longer than I thought you would. Where did you get that bear?"

"You timed me?" The idea irritated her, but she didn't have time to waste her mini-break on grousing about it. "Slade didn't kill his wife."

The door popped opened, and two middle-aged women visitors stepped on. Donna wanted to finish the conversation and shuffled closer to Mark. "I was right."

"Didn't say you weren't."

"Come to my car. I have something you might like."

They got off at the parking garage stop only to hear one of the women comment. "My mother always told me nurses were easy. She was right."

Mark had the nerve to laugh at the comment while Donna puffed up. "If they had any clue at how hard nurses work, they'd know there was no time for hanky-panky. Stupid medical dramas ruining everyone's perception of nurses."

Mark put his hands out in front of him. "Hey, you don't have to convince me."

"Okay. I went out to where Summer was shot and the car wrecked."

"Of course you did."

She ignored his comment and continued. "That's where I picked up the bear. I only picked it up because Tennyson commented on Kee Kee declaring herself Summer's number one fan and I saw the note. Sometimes, she attacked Summer's rivals on social media. To me, she sounded like a probable candidate."

Mark cocked his head to the side and fixed her with the same disbelieving stare Jasper used when she mentioned a bath. "She's a fan."

"I know that. Plenty of people have been shot at by their own fans. Besides, Slade told me that Summer commented that Kee Kee used her fan status to get closer to the husband as opposed to the singer."

"Interesting. So how do you go about finding someone just named Kee Kee?"

"It's an alias. It has to be since she threatens so many people publicly. I have the note she wrote and stuck on the bear. I didn't handle it so you should be able to get fingerprints off it."

"Good girl." He rubbed his hands together in delight and patted his jacket down for a plastic evidence bag. He pulled out the bag and blew into it. That way the prints wouldn't be smeared as he put the letter inside.

"Did you read the letter?"

Donna pulled the key fob out of her purse and pushed it. "Only the outside. I had no time after visiting the local lovers' lane and dealing with an intense fan who may or may not be Kee Kee."

The detective's face went all stone on her before he managed to push out the words. "Start at the beginning."

It wasn't her finest sleuth moment, but if he insisted. "When I saw the tumble-down barn, I thought it would be a good place to wait for Summer. That meant knowing she'd be traveling on Route 17 at that time. Anyhow, I walked on the grass so as not to disturb the tire prints, but there were too many of them. When I reached the barn, and discovered the beer bottles, quilt, and stubby candle, I figured it was…" Mark made a slashing gesture with his hand, causing Donna to stumble to a stop in mid-sentence, which was just as well.

"Not that story, the one about Kee Kee."

"Oh, that one. Not too sure it was Kee Kee. Then again, maybe it was." She ignored Mark's hurry-up sign. If he wanted to hear her story, then he'd have to let her tell it her way. "When I first saw the woman crying at the memorial, I assumed she was just another fan.

It wasn't my intention to bother her, but that darn bear started talking. For a while, she was okay because she assumed she was getting some divine message from Summer. Then she went ballistic when it mentioned Kee Kee's name."

"Wait," Mark interrupted her. "I thought you said the woman was Kee Kee. Why would she get upset by Kee Kee's name?"

"Ah, you're missing it. Let's assume Kee Kee isn't the most stable chick around. Slade remembered her as being intense, slender, dark hair, and stuck on him. The woman I saw had dark hair, on the skinny side, and Lord Have Mercy, she was intense. Are you with me so far?"

Mark circled two fingers, which she took to mean yes as opposed to wind it up. "Anyhow, let's say Kee Kee did kill Summer. She feels regret, which explains why she said Kee Kee wasn't a true fan. She left a box by the memorial, which would have her fingerprints on it. You could compare them to the note."

"True. It's a good plan. Now, I have to trust that not everyone and his brother handled the box."

The dig that she'd handled it didn't bother her since she hadn't. "I only kept the bear because of Kee Kee's name. As soon as I heard about the shooting, I suspected a fan."

"Why is that?"

It was her turn to give Mark a blank stare. *Really, he didn't know.* "The line between love and obsession can blur at times."

Chapter Eighteen

D ONNA TRIED TO put herself in Kee Kee's mindset. Did she mean to kill Summer? She assumed she did, but if it wasn't deliberate, what if she wanted it to appear as if a rival had targeted her? It would blow up publicity-wise and make all her rivals look guilty even when they weren't.

Could be the shooter wasn't that experienced and thought she shot above or around as opposed to directly at Summer. There was an outside chance that the shooter didn't even know she was shooting at Summer, which only left Slade. Why would a fan want to kill the husband?

A male fan might fancy taking his place. A female fan might feel like Slade didn't pay enough attention to his wife. In the short time he'd been at the hospital, females of all ages were practically doing backflips to please him. When two women visitors left room twelve holding hands, an iconic light bulb lit over her head. Oh yeah, a female fan could be just as much in love with Summer as a male fan.

A fragment of her dream materialized in her mind. Summer had on a black watch cap and aviator sunglasses. No makeup, no earrings that suggested they left in a rush, already late for the appearance. What if the killer mistook Summer for Slade? It was hard to believe someone could make such an egregious error, but the windows were tinted and the car was traveling at a high rate of speed. At best, the shooter had only seconds to catch up to the car, aim, shoot, and get away. Imagine the horror the person might have felt to find out she shot the object of her obsession. Not only would it make her not a true fan, but also it would make her angry, possibly angry enough to finish off Slade.

The man was sitting unguarded in his room. Since his memory had come back, his television was now functioning. Slade could be watching a lame reality show when his world ended. Donna jogged the few steps into the room only to find her patient reading. He looked up at Donna's entrance.

"Hey. Have you ever read this book?" He held up *Gone with the Wind* with his finger marking his place.

"Not sure if there is a girl south of the Mason-Dixon line who hasn't. Why?"

"Scarlett in the story really goes after what she wants. I have to admire that." He grinned, turned the book up in his lap, and flipped a page. "The story pulled me back in."

She imagined Kee Kee was just as determined as Scarlett. Would Slade admire her when she shot him? Probably not, people tended to feel differently when they were personally involved.

Technically, the hospital had security, but in the loosest sense of the word. If a person parked too long in a designated spot, usually a doctor's or the emergency lane, their vehicle ended up towed. Every now and then, a homeless person or traveler wandered into the lobby at night. For the most part, the guards ignored them when they stretched out on the long, leather couches and slept. They usually woke the visitors before the first shift arrived. Often Donna surprised sleepers and guards both when she'd arrived earlier than expected for her first shift.

Whenever out-of-control patient or antagonistic ex showed up, it took forever for security to arrive. They stayed mainly near the emergency room where the most colorful patients showed up, tending to arrive more on full-moon nights. The higher the floor the less likely security would get there in time. The hospital's recent influx of orderlies who could have come from the professional wrestling circuit helped some. When all else failed, Donna could out bluff most suspicious characters. She couldn't outmaneuver a gun, though.

What they needed was a cop outside the door. Sure, criminals always outsmarted the cop in the television shows, but they often had alien DNA and crawled up the side of the building. A run-of-the-mill obsessive fan would spot the cop and decide to try another day.

She rounded the corner and waved at Shelley. "I'm back."

"Did you send your man in blue off with a big sloppy kiss?" Shelley added smooching sounds.

Geesh, how old was this woman? "I think we waved at one another."

"You might as well have stayed up here then. What is wrong with the two of you? Do you think you're going to live forever?"

More than once, she'd analyzed Mark's behavior, trying to decide if he liked her or her cheesecake. The dessert earned a definite yes, but as for Donna, she wasn't so sure, even though he had acted jealous about Thomas. Men could be difficult to understand. It never occurred to her that something was wrong with her. She rather liked it all being on Mark, even though she knew better. "You have some inspired suggestions?"

"Invite him over for Christmas. He's single. Kids?"

She shook her head no. The man would have been a great father or even grandfather. "He'll probably volunteer to work Christmas."

"Christmas is twenty-four hours. I suspect he won't work the entire day. You're a great cook. You live in this gorgeous Victorian mansion. You're practically a special Christmas setting. Have a fire. Put on some tunes. Move your stalled romance forward."

Donna wanted to deny there was a romance, stalled or otherwise, but Shelley gave her an innocuous reason to call Mark. "What a great idea. I need to call him right away."

"There are plenty of empty rooms."

Shelley didn't officially give her another break, but pointed out the obvious. "I think I'll check on a patient."

Donna looked in on a patient, suiting her actions to her words, before slipping off to an empty room. She moved far enough from the open door to not be overheard. Mark was three on her speed dial.

"Missed me already?" he teased when he answered the phone.

"In a way." She remembered her mother's admonishment about delivering honey before the vinegar. "I wanted to know if you were free anytime on Christmas."

"Is this a special invite to Tollhouse Christmas festivities?" There was a jovial note to his voice.

"I can't say how many Tollhouses will be there. Maria and Daniel could celebrate on their own, but might show up later for dinner. Hard to tell with my mother. She has so many suitors; one of them might provide a grand holiday."

"She might want a break from that, too."

"Could be. There will be Tennyson. It will be his first official Christmas."

"I must come then. I love the way a kid's eyes light up on Christmas morning. Any suggestions what the boy would like?"

"A girlfriend."

"It's easier buying for the younger ones."

"True, so should I count you as a yes?"

"Absolutely. Dare I hope there will be cheesecake?"

"Whatever I make, you'll like it."

"Always do."

"I have another favor."

"Here it comes."

"Stop that. Was Summer wearing a heavy dark jacket, a black watch cap, and aviator sunglasses when she was brought in?"

"How did you know?" She didn't feel up to sharing her dreams for the incredulity it'd draw. "I have my sources. Anyhow, I have reason to believe that Summer wasn't the target. Slade was. Could be the killer may try to finish what he or she didn't accomplish with the first shot. Would it be possible to assign an officer for security?"

"Already have. I had similar thoughts. Slade was okay as long as he didn't remember anything. Now that he's coherent, word will get out, which should shake up our murderer. With any luck, we might catch her slipping into Slade's room."

"That would make him a sitting duck." While this ploy had worked successfully in many police dramas, Donna recognized reality varied a great deal from the televised one. For one thing, her hospital was not full of hot doctors and nurses. She'd had more than one patient complain about that particular lack, usually the little old ladies.

"Oh, it might if we were dealing with a professional, but it looks more and more like a prank that went wrong. If it is Kee Kee, our accidental killer will ball up her courage to confront Slade. Remember, we're talking about a man in his prime who could easily overpower a young woman. Even so, she won't get that far. We'll have an undercover cop downstairs, and the hospital has security cameras that help monitor everything."

Legacy didn't have the biggest police force, and it would be hard to dedicate several officers during a bare bones roster that often occurred during the holiday season when everyone tried to use their vacation days. Besides, the only cars on the road were heading to grandmother's house.

"I'm not a fan of this plan."

Mark's reply bordered on terse. "It's not your plan."

Sure, he complained when she pointed out a procedure she thought was asinine or that wouldn't work. Despite being a thirty-year veteran, he should be open to new ideas. Donna counted herself lucky he even took the note, but to her, Kee Kee as a culprit just made sense. Not every murder was deliberate, not every killer was a sociopath, but she did have some doubts about the woman who recorded the creepy messages for the bear voice box.

"My plan would be better, more complex." No way she could let him get away with discounting any advice she might have given.

A snort sounded in her ear that could have been a throat clearing or something slightly derogatory before he teased, "I imagine there would be no less than five people involved in it with at least two of them being family members. Disguises would be used too."

His words sparked a plan. One Mark wouldn't approve of, but all the same, it would protect Slade. The good-natured man had grown on her, and it had nothing to do with his stellar good looks. "Relatives are the easiest to convince, and they work free. I can pull it off with four people, counting myself."

A panicky note slipped into his voice. "Donna, you aren't planning anything, are you?"

"My Christmas tea is only four days away followed by the actual holiday. I have too much to do to be up to something." It wasn't an outright lie. Besides, she might not need to shift her plan into gear at all, but it was good to be ready.

"You didn't answer my question."

"Mark, I'm at work. As much as I love to talk, one of the patients is pushing the nurse button. Gotta go." She thumbed the phone off before the man could even give her a rushed goodbye. It wasn't as if he had never ended a conversation abruptly.

Out in the hall, an officer in a blue police officer uniform stood by Slade's door. At least Mark wasn't going for the subtle angle. Still, Donna gave the standing man a thorough once-over. His uniform appeared to be standard issue along with his gear belt and gun. He could have clubbed the original officer and taken his clothes. She should be able to ask to see his ID. If he didn't look like it, then she would know. If he hesitated, that would be another clue. He did have a gun and if she confronted him, he could shoot her, which would blow his cover, but he could still take Slade hostage as his way out of the hospital.

Donna inhaled deeply, trusting this would not be the last impulsive thing she did. Tennyson deserved to have a decent Christmas. Even though she knew she should have a will, she'd never bothered, assuming she'd live another twenty or thirty years. The cop was only six feet away when she slowed to a stop. Did she really want to make this big of a challenge without thinking it through?

Shelley bustled up behind her. "Oh, there you are. As you can see, we now have security. Let me introduce you."

The head nurse smiled at the very young man trying to look stern with his super short haircut and smooth baby-faced features. He couldn't pull it off. His stern expression made him look more like a pouting cherub. Shelley gestured to the man. "Meet Gunnar Jorgenson. His mother, Hilda, works in housekeeping."

There were easily over a hundred people who worked full time in the hospital. Housekeeping usually kept to their basement quarters filled with noisy dryers and oversized washers, but she could remember a blond woman occasionally showing up with the clean linen cart. Might be his mother. They did little more than nod at each other. "Good woman," she stated, which made the officer in question smile, making him look even younger if that were even possible.

"That's my mother."

Donna held out her hand. "Pleased to meet you. Are you a new academy graduate?"

He grasped hers in a firm grip and gave it a hearty shake before releasing it. "Not as new as you might think. It has been five years. It's the curse of being a natural blond that makes me look so much younger than my age. When I graduated, there was some talk about me going back to high school to bust drug sellers."

"Did you?"

Gunnar gave a dramatic shudder. "Thankfully, no. I wouldn't want to take calculus again. Barely passed the first time."

"You'd actually have to do the classwork?"

"Some of it. I wouldn't have to be a superior student, but I couldn't excuse myself if we had a test that day."

"Guess you lucked out they didn't pick you." Donna's internal thoughts were at war with her actual words. Mark put someone who barely made it out of high school on security. A bat of the eyelashes, a low neckline, or a compliment could have the man granting entrance. Depending on Kee Kee's intelligence, she could come dressed as a doctor, except Donna knew every doctor here, even the visiting ones. Slade didn't know if the culprit was young or middle-aged.

Donna stepped around the officer to open the door, but found

Gunnar's hand was already there. "Your business, ma'am?"

The fact she was wearing scrubs and was in the hospital should have made it self-evident. "I'm checking on my patient."

"As I suspected. I'll accompany you."

Well, this wasn't what she wanted. The extra precautions were probably thanks to the good detective. She gritted her teeth as she followed the officer. Slade sat up in bed, flipping channels with the remote. Soap operas flickered on the television screen, only to be replaced by the news, then some talk show with people pushing each other and yelling profanities indicated by the numerous beeps. The screen flickered before it went black.

Slade put the remote down with a sigh and looked up at Donna. "I thought watching television would jog my memory. There's still so many things I don't remember, but everything on it is so negative. People cheating on the ones they love, employees stealing from their companies, terrorists, natural disasters and…" Slade paused, making sure he had Donna's attention. "…there is one entire show devoted to finding out who's the baby's daddy since the momma has no clue."

"Ah yeah, I'm familiar with that one." Donna's eyebrows went up since she felt her acknowledgment implied she was a fan. "Not that I watch it." At least, not after the first time, mainly due to her need to have a higher respect for her fellow human.

"Then," Slade held up a hand, "there's a show where these men compete to have a woman fall in love with them. How in the world can she truly love one when she's dating all of them?"

Gunnar met her eyes and shrugged. Obviously, she was on her own with that question. "I don't think it's real, even though they call it a reality show. People on the show act a certain way to improve ratings. You and Summer were in show business. Didn't you do anything to improve your public image?"

Slade blinked, his fingers smoothed his eyebrows and continued across his forehead. "We did something that we didn't mean, to make ourselves more appealing to the general public?"

"Yeah. That's about it." Unfortunately, his lost-boy expression meant she wouldn't get any usable information today. Could be they gave him a sedative to relax him, but it could have made his already hazy memories harder to recall.

When she figured it was all a wasted effort, especially with Gunnar as her personal watchdog, Slade spoke. His demeanor changed from the slightly confused, *I'm new to this planet* demeanor to a weary individual who'd experienced more than he liked. "We got married." Slade reached for the remote and flicked the television back on, refusing to elaborate.

Chapter Nineteen

G UNNAR CLOSED THE door behind them and shot her an enigmatic look. Normally, she'd take the time to analyze it, but not now, not when her theory crumbled under three words, *we got married.* Their marriage must not have been a happy union. It didn't mean they hadn't dated. An opportunistic manager decided a wedding would push sales, especially if a wedding song or a love duo showed up on the latest album. Could Slade sing?

The rest of the day passed in a blur as she tried to imagine Slade as a killer. Logistically the shot had come from outside the car, but he could have hired someone. "No, I refuse to accept it."

The petite white-haired lady peeped over her cooking magazine. "What won't you accept?"

She hadn't meant to say that aloud. "I refuse to believe Santa isn't real. Too many people want to stamp out the magic that jolly old elf symbolizes." Donna placed her splayed hand over her heart. "I'm a believer."

The woman dropped her magazine and mirrored Donna's actions. "I believe, too. What do you want Santa to bring you?"

Good question. One she hadn't considered in years. A sewn-up criminal case didn't have the same ring as a Caribbean vacation even if it was what she wanted. "This year I'd like..." She stalled as she searched her mind for the various kitchen appliances she lusted after and rejected as too impractical. "I want all those I love together for an old-fashioned Christmas."

The woman clapped her hands together. "Well said. Obviously, you're a young woman of sense and sensibility. It takes people forever to understand what really matters is what is in here." Her cupped hand touched her chest where her heart resided. "Enjoy. I envy you."

Donna touched the tablet mounted on the wall to access Evelyn Buchannan's records. "It looks to me like you'll be out of here in plenty of time to celebrate the holiday."

Instead of looking overjoyed at the prospect, the woman's face puckered as if she'd bitten into something particularly distasteful. "I'd rather be here than back at the nursing home. They push everyone into the dining room where they have a skinny artificial tree that's missing branches. It looks more like a hat rack than an evergreen. Some business, maybe a scout troop, wraps up one present for each of us. Usually, it's talcum powder or socks. Last year, I got some of those extra tall tube socks that didn't stay up. One of the employees dresses up as Santa in a cheap polyester suit. It's all so sad. The food is the worst. Usually, it's some pureed nastiness. Last year, someone in dietary thought putting in green food coloring would make it more festive." Evelyn grimaced. "I won't even tell you what it looked like."

The back of her neck ached as Donna listened intently. Her hand eased up to rub her neck while she imagined the dismal holiday party. No one should celebrate Christmas Day in such a painful manner. "Could you get out if someone invited you somewhere?"

"I could if my son approved it."

She had a son and still had to tolerate the budget holiday cele-bration. "Does your son live close by?"

If he lived on the West Coast or a foreign country, she'd give him a pass. Even so, he could fly.

"He lives in Ashville. At least, he used to. He just married wife number four. Tiffani might find North Carolina not to her tastes."

"Could we call him and tell him you're spending Christmas with me and my family?"

Her eyes lit up as her hands came together in front of her chest. "That sounds like fun. Do you have a real tree?"

"I do. Even better, I can cook. If you arrived before Christmas Eve, you might even meet Santa."

"Oh my goodness." Mrs. Buchannan waved her hand in front of her face as if overcome. "You're such a sweetie. I can't wait. Do you have children?"

"Well, there's Tennyson. He can be childlike at times. There's my dog, Jasper. Are you allergic to dogs?"

"Good heavens, no." She beamed as she bounced on her bed. "I can't believe it. I used to have a little terrier. My son got rid of it when he decided I needed to go in the home."

Someone should tell the ungrateful son a thing or two. That person would probably be her when she called up. First, she had to get permission for the visit. "I'm so sorry you ended up in the home, but we can make this holiday festive. I'm even having a Victorian tea at my place."

"Wonderful!"

"Your son's number?"

Mrs. Buchannan blinked her faded blue eyes and made a surprised O with her lips. "I don't know. I should know. He keeps changing it and tells me not to call. Right now, he and Tiffani are on an extended honeymoon cruise throughout Europe. My son told me not to bother to call since his phone won't work on the cruise and all." Her brows lowered even more. "I think he said that. I forget things. That's why I'm in the home."

"Everyone forgets things. No worries, I'll contact the home and will figure it out." One more person, especially the forgotten, elderly sweetheart, would make little difference in her plans.

The detail tweaking for her Victorian tea and planning a special Christmas that Tennyson and Evelyn would never forget consumed her attention. Well, most of it, when she wasn't doing actual nursing duties or worrying that her plan with Slade could massively backfire.

Shelley caught up to her in the hall. They kept pace as they walked back to the nurses' station. The woman leaned slightly in Donna's direction as she spoke. "Today is your turn to leave something for Kathy from her Secret Santa."

Oh sugar! Donna had come up with the idea to give the weary mother a lift. It didn't work out well if she didn't do her part. "Got it." Well, she didn't have it. Any sweets from the hospital cafeteria would be far from special. The gift shop had a generic assortment of teddy bears with slightly perplexed expressions as if not quite sure how they ended up there. Kathy would recognize any of the gift shop flowers or balloons. It might as well have stenciled *Lazy Secret Santa* on it. What could she give the woman that wasn't lame?

She opened her oversized purse looking for something other than a pack of tissues and a half-used pack of mints. The unopened expensive hand cream her mother gifted her would work. "I have the perfect item, although I should type a note to fool her."

Too bad all her issues couldn't be solved that easily. Thursday was the Victorian tea, which Robert had tentatively agreed to attend. Half of the nibbles were already in the freezer. Saturday was Christmas Eve, which she'd originally agreed to work.

The real question would be if she should sneak Slade out before the killer showed. If she did get him out, where would he stay? Mark wasn't going to like this one little bit. It might result in her not getting a Christmas present. Of course, that would depend on him getting her one to begin with. Her instincts told her something was afoot. Her instincts weren't known for being specific, though.

Chapter Twenty

A FIRE GLOWED in the parlor fireplace, consuming the expensive ash logs Donna bought for the occasion. Nutmeg and cinnamon sprinkled on the logs contributed to a more festive scent. The tree took center stage with its height, width, and multi-colored lights. The train her mother bought chugged around the tree, fascinating at least two of the visitors.

One preschool girl, festooned in a velvet dress and green hair bow, pointed to the train. "What does it say?"

The older boy leaned forward, possibly trying to make sense of the symbols Donna had concluded were Russian. He gave the girl a dismissive glance and announced, "Big brothers get more presents than little sisters."

The girl gave a peremptory wail, which indicated her intentions to pitch a hissy fit.

Maria showed up in an elf costume that fascinated the girl enough that she forgot about the perfidy of her brother. Her sister-in-law entertained the munchkins with elf lore while Tennyson and she trotted out platters of goodies. Her mother showed up with her instant camera and packs of film. Donna didn't even know they still made instant developing film. Still, it was a good deal if the photos turned out well. Each happy mother or grandmother would have a souvenir of their personal darling's visit with Santa. A couple of the younger grandmothers might insist on a photo with the old elf themselves.

While still in the kitchen, Tennyson argued against the practice of children sitting on Santa's lap, insisting it made children easy targets for bearded old men. After all, their parents urged them every year to climb onto a stranger's lap and ask for presents. It seemed like a perfect setup. The boy had never experienced climbing into Santa's lap, believing a simple request to deliver a present by an innocent child could result in roller skates under the tree. It was magic. Sure, the magic often had a great deal to do with parents doing without to provide a nice holiday for the family.

Donna pushed the tea trolley in last. She wanted to be the one to handle the hot water. She'd gladly pour every cup of tea to prevent any accidents. She even came up with the idea of souvenir plastic mugs for the children, complete with tops and bendable straws. When her brother pointed out it wasn't exactly Victorian, she'd acknowledged not everything could be period. The soft instrumental music playing in the background wasn't exactly Victorian either, except for a few familiar hymns.

Soft laughter, feminine chatter, and the occasional "how precious" when their child crawled into Santa's lap filled the room. For today, Robert left his red suit upstairs. He wore forest green knickers with a red checked shirt and an embroidered vest that had tiny reindeer and snowflakes in gold against the black fabric. What intrigued the children most were his buckled shoes, evergreen knee socks, and pocket watch. They had no issues recognizing him without the hat or fur-trimmed coat.

One well-dressed matron cornered Donna. *Here it comes. Something isn't period perfect.*

"Oh my, I had to tell you how wonderful everything is. It's the perfect balance. I like the relaxed atmosphere. This is the only time my little Benjamin has ever climbed onto Santa's lap. Those mall stand-ins can have a tinge of the sordid about them."

Donna wanted to point out that what the woman smelled was the result of various babies and toddlers wetting on the mall Santas. Instead, she smiled. "I'm so glad you like it. I might make it into an annual event."

"Please do." The woman patted Donna's arm before turning away.

The clatter of a cane on the stairs indicated someone descending, but everyone was here except for Evelyn. The son she thought wouldn't give permission was more than happy for his mother to spend Christmas with her. David, the son, also added that he wasn't married or on his honeymoon. As for living nearby, his company had stationed him in Dubai. He was glad his mother had someone to make sure she had a nice time. Just before bidding her goodbye, he mentioned her tenuous grasp on reality. He should have led with that one.

The tiny woman was dressed in a long, elaborate white lace gown with a train sliding down the stairs behind her. A sparkly tiara decorated her upswept hair, which would make her the envy of every little girl present. Her long white gloves went to her elbows. In her right hand, she held a quizzing glass on a gilded wand.

People turned and whispered while Evelyn motioned for someone. Tennyson was the closest and reached her first. She whispered something into his ear, which caused him to throw an apologetic glance at Donna. Evelyn landed an elbow in the boy's rib, causing him to clear his throat.

"It is my honor to introduce the lost princess, Anastasia."

Robert worked his way through the staring people to the counterfeit princess's side. He bowed deeply. "Your imperial highness.

May I have the honor?" He held out a bent arm. Evelyn took it with an aristocratic hauteur. They made their way around the room with many of the girls offering their best curtsies.

Donna watched, waiting for something else to happen, but Evelyn never broke character. The grandmothers beamed at their children's decorous behavior in the presence of royalty, even if it was pretend.

It was almost over when the local reporter arrived for photos. He managed to get a few sound bites from happy partygoers before a yellow cab stopped in front of her house, too late for the party. A man in a red Santa suit jumped out. Some of the children pointed and looked back at Robert. One boy shouted, "Do something. It's the evil Santa."

To affirm his claim, the cabbie yelled out the window. "You forgot to pay me."

"Santa is a crook!" the same annoying boy shouted.

Robert held up his hand. "I'll handle this. I'll go see if he is one of my helpers."

Donna watched the man in the red suit dart up the steps, but stop when he saw the crowd on the porch. The startled well-arched eyebrows rang a bell. *Slade.* She made eye contact with him and angled her head to the left. With any luck, he'd go to the side door.

Robert paid the cab driver and got the crowd laughing about good help being so hard to find. On the side stoop, she found Slade sweating.

She pulled him into the kitchen and pushed him toward a stool. "Sit. I'll get you something to drink."

"A vodka double."

Donna placed a glass of water in front of him. "What happened? I told you the suit was only for an emergency."

"Trust me. It was." He pulled down the fake beard and drank the entire glass. "Can I have the vodka now?"

He held out his hand, and it trembled. "I need something stronger." There was petulance to his tone, which might be as close to the real Slade as she'd ever experienced.

She poured a mug of coffee and slid it across the counter. "Much stronger than water. Explain." She put both hands on her hips, unsure if the reporter had taken a snapshot of the fleeing Santa, which wasn't the image she wanted for her Victorian Tea.

"I thought everything was fine until I heard voices outside the door. The woman's voice was familiar. She kept insisting she was my sister. The officer laughed, said something about her not looking like me. She called him a fool and explained not all siblings resembled one another."

It was easy to picture Slade lying on his hospital bed listening to the conversation. "At what point did you get worried?"

"Probably when she insisted I had a sister. I'm an only child. Technically, since both my parents are dead, I'm an orphan. Even with the suit on, I didn't have any way out, but your hospital is old enough to have windows that open. Saved my butt."

"You were on the fifth floor!"

"Tell me about it." He wiped his brow. "I won't lie. I was scared. There was some scaffolding I managed to make my way to by shuffling along the ledge and holding onto the brick." He held out his abraded hands.

"We'll need to take care of your hands before they get infected. Why did you run? Did you have any reason to think the woman meant to harm you?"

Slade had picked up his coffee, but put it back down. "You were the one who told me I might be in danger. Some chick who sounds familiar, is desperate to get in my room, and lies about being my sister. Sounds suspicious to me."

"Could be a fan." There had been previous women who tried to get into his room.

He scratched the back of his neck. "I don't think so. I'm an underwear model. My fans don't usually recognize my face. When I do meet them, they're all giggly and tend to run in packs. This woman was intense and alone."

"You could have a point. Here's what I'm going to do." She tried to think of everyone she had in the house. There were the Dickens, Robert, Evelyn, and Tennyson. Her mother might stay for Christmas Eve so as not to spend her first Christmas alone. Putting him in a room might not be a problem, but people seeing him could be. "Okay, I'll put you in a third-story bedroom that has an access door to the attic. When in doubt, go upward. I'll bring you up food, but stay in the room and keep it locked until told otherwise."

Slade glanced at the leftover platters strewn about the kitchen. "I wouldn't mind some of that with a bottle of vodka."

"Yeah, but a man on the run can't afford to get tipsy. Besides, didn't your agent tell you drinking puts on the weight?"

The man shrugged. Donna went to the interior door and spotted Tennyson. "Lock the front door." Her employee gave her an *Are You Crazy* stare.

She held up her hand. "Five seconds, then unlock it."

Donna grabbed Slade's arm and gave it a good yank. "Let's go while no one can see you. Already, some of my tea participants may be talking about Santa stiffing the cab driver. If someone is chasing you, she might make it this far."

"You were the one with the great idea about the Santa suit."

"I can understand why someone wanted to shoot you." She

hadn't meant the comment as a mean one, but it stopped Slade.

"It was me they were trying to kill?" He darted across the foyer and took the stairs, two at once.

Donna told Tennyson to open the door before following Slade. She'd already told him more than once someone could be trying to kill him. If he hadn't believed her, why did he do his own version of doing everything a spider can? It made no sense. Could be Slade was a handsome shell without much inside. As she passed the check-in desk, she grabbed the key she needed.

She climbed the three sets of stairs, not once, twice, or even three times, but four times, taking Slade food and clothes borrowed from Tennyson's room. She doubted her employee would want to wear them again, which meant a little something extra in his stocking.

After her last trip up the stairs, she leaned against the newel post at the end of the stairs to catch her breath. Maria and Tennyson were tidying up while Robert chatted with her mother. The bell at the front door jangled violently with Mark's entrance.

"Where is he?"

Evelyn drifted in from the dining room. She tapped Mark sharply on the shoulder with her quizzing glass. "You will not speak to my serf in such a manner."

He stepped sideways, making sure he was out of tapping range. "Who is that?"

Tennyson carried a platter of empty china teacups past the flustered detective. "Her imperial highness, the Princess Anastasia."

"Donna, I need to talk to you."

Evelyn slid closer and held up her quizzing glass stick. "Please moderate your tone."

His face blanched as he directed an annoyed glance at Evelyn. Mark coughed, then backed up to the wall. His hand pressed against his chest as beads of sweat popped out on his forehead. Weird, since the door still stood open, allowing the frosty air inside.

He winced and half-whispered, "Help me," and slid down the wall.

Chapter Twenty-One

ROBERT REACHED MARK first, catching him by the arm before he hit the floor. It only took a second for Donna's training to kick in. "Mom, get the baby aspirin from the kitchen." She knelt beside the wild-eyed man, taking his pulse, which was thready. An upward glance confirmed Tennyson was calling for an ambulance without even being asked. Thank the Good Lord for that.

Years in the emergency room had her operating on autopilot, but it didn't stop her own heart from racing. Her mother's heels clattered as she rushed back. She stumbled, spilling the chewable aspirins all over the floor. "Oh no!"

"All I need is one. I'm sure you have one." Donna spoke slow and calm, feeling anything but. Everyone would look to her for guidance as the medical professional. She took the aspirin Cecilia handed her, crumbled it a bit, and placed the residue under Mark's tongue. She smoothed his hair off his clammy brow.

"Donna," he managed in a gasp.

"Don't talk. It's going to be okay." In the distance, the distinctive whine of an ambulance wailed.

Mark tried to grin, but winced instead. "Always thought a bullet would take me out."

She placed her finger against his lips, not wanting to hear what he might say. "Hush. It's okay. I'll make sure they put you on my ward so I can keep my eye on you."

A squeal of tires sounded and vehicle doors slammed. The front door still stood open, allowing Donna to watch the paramedic sprint up the stairs, medic kit in her hand. The woman stepped in the door, her gaze sweeping the room for the patient. Donna waved her down. Thank goodness it was Lana, one of her favorite medics. The woman reminded her of bit of herself, except she was twenty years younger.

"What happened?" Lana knelt beside Mark and pulled out her stethoscope. She handed the blood pressure gauge to Donna. "You do it."

Donna attached the cuff as Lana unbuttoned Mark's shirt. His eyes were watchful, a good sign he was still coherent. His blood pressure was low as she suspected. "How's the heart?"

Instead of answering, Lana offered her the stethoscope. Smart of her, not talking in front of the patient. Donna placed the earpieces in her ears, certain of what she would hear. The heartbeat was too slow and weak. Her panicked eyes met Lana's. "He's a smoker." The underlying message remained unspoken. His ability to bounce back had been compromised by a thoughtless addiction.

The other medic came in with the metallic clang of the gurney. He nodded at Donna and glanced at his partner.

"Presents as a heart attack. We need to get him to the hospital pronto. I'll ride in the back. You drive."

Donna glanced from Lana to the other medic, Jordan. "There's only two of you?

Jordan maneuvered the gurney beside Mark. "Yes." Jordan placed his hands under Mark's shoulders, lifting him slightly to maneuver a long board under him. The two medics strapped him down while Donna hovered after them wringing her hands. This wasn't supposed to happen, especially when things were rough between the two of them.

She stepped back to allow the medics access to the gurney. "I can ride in the ambulance."

Jordan shook his head. "It's against regulations. You can follow us to the hospital."

Mark's voice came out scratchy and low, forcing the three of them to bend low to hear.

"Don't argue with her. You won't win."

It was all she could do not to roll her eyes, but she was riding in the ambulance, come hell or high water. "I'm an experienced nurse, not a hysterical spouse."

Lana motioned for Jordan to go. Donna followed behind carrying the medic kit. Mark's eyes fluttered shut as they lifted him into the back. Unconsciousness wasn't unexpected. Lana started oxygen while Donna attached the electrodes. The ambulance took a hard right, causing her to tumble against the wall. At least Mark was strapped in. The ride to the hospital was probably the longest and shortest of her life.

At the emergency room, they forced Donna into the waiting room with all the other uninformed relatives and friends. She paced the room, looking up every time the doors opened. The room was only eighteen by twelve feet. She counted it off repeatedly as she walked. A television mounted high in the corner blared out some dreary news story. Most of the magazines were missing covers. Even though a large, no smoking symbol decorated the wall, the ghost of cigarette smoke hung over the place. The urge to kick something or at least fling one of the magazines across the room stalled as her family poured through the entrance.

Her mother, brother, sister-in-law, even Tennyson and Robert completed the group. It made her wonder who was at the inn. "Who's taking care of the inn?"

Maria answered. "The Dickens are going to stay the night with their son so you won't have to worry about anything. Janice agreed to swing by since The Croaking Frog was closing early for the holidays."

"That was nice of the Dickens, but I ah, need someone at the Inn." Donna sucked in her lips wondering who she could get to check out the place. Janice's promise to come by didn't reassure her, especially since she'd been privy to several conversations with the restaurant owner that started just when Donna was ready to leave. She stared at each person, contemplating how she could get them to go check on the inn. Maria would have faith that Janice would show up. Mark and Daniel had gotten to be pretty close. Tennyson would insist Mark was a second father to him. Her mother had no real interest in Mark, especially when she hinted that Donna should give up on the man.

"Mom, could you stop by the inn, just to check on Evelyn? She's all alone, you know." She had her fingers crossed behind her back hoping her mother would take the bait.

Her mother reached out to enclose Donna's hand in hers. "I'm here for you, honey. Tell you what, I'll call Herman. That's what I'll do."

Cecilia dropped Donna's hand to dial her phone. After a few quick instructions, she smiled. "I believe I may have stirred up a romance. Herman was asking me if Evelyn was a looker and single."

Officer Wells entered the waiting room and took a seat. She nodded at the fresh-faced officer she'd met during her class reunion murder case.

"I heard about Detective Taber on the radio. He's always there for everyone else. I figured I could be here for him."

"That's really sweet of you. Did anyone call Mark's sister?"

Her mother nodded. "I did. She's on her way. She wasn't even that far away."

She'd heard a great deal about the sister, but had never met her. The one thing she did know was the woman liked haunted bed and breakfasts. With any luck, The Painted Lady Inn wouldn't be haunted by her brother.

A white-haired doctor came through the doors. "Who's here for Mark Taber?"

They all stood up.

The doctor nodded. "Okay, then. He's stable. We're going to keep him for observation tonight. It will be a while before you can see him."

The older doctor glanced at Donna and smiled. "I believe there was a request for Nurse Tollhouse's services."

"More likely he begged you not to put him on my floor."

"No, come with me. It'll be a short visit, but I think seeing you will ease his mind. It will probably help him get better faster."

No one had ever accused her of being a cure-all. "Let's go."

Dr. Douglas led her through the rabbit warren of rooms and cubicles that made up the ER. "Heard you rode in the ambulance. That's against the rules."

"I know."

She expected something else, perhaps a write-up in her personnel file.

He gave a slight chuckle. "I would have done the same if my dear wife were on the way to the hospital." A technician exited a curtained area and nodded at the doctor. "He's in there." She could hear Wells complaining that he needed to see Taber, too.

At least she got in front of Wells. The bed had been cranked into a sitting position. Wires from electrodes hung suspended in the area between Mark's chest and a nearby monitor. The steady beep assured her his heart was working. His head bent over his narrow notepad as he wrote something.

"I see you're hard at work." It shouldn't have surprised her. The man only took a few minutes out for a life-threatening heart attack.

"Donna. I'm grateful the doctor took me seriously when I said I had to see you." He marked out something on his notebook, then glanced back up. "I had an officer tasered and I assume Slade is the culprit."

How could the man get it so wrong? She decided this wouldn't be the best time to point it out. "Slade snuck out his window when he heard a voice he recognized arguing with the officer outside his door. I even lent him a Santa suit in case he needed to escape."

"That would explain the call about Santa climbing the hospital walls."

"Probably. What about Kee Kee? Did she get away?"

Mark took a deep breath and coughed.

"Don't talk if it's too hard." She reached for his free hand and interlaced her fingers with his.

"No, I may be sidelined, but I trust you and Wells can finish what I started. Kee Kee was a wash. We did find her from her fingerprints."

Donna had been sure she was the one. "Why? She put all those threatening notes on social media and left that creepy bear."

"True. She's also eleven. Her fingerprints were in the base as part of Child Find. She didn't mean anything by the notes. She was having fun on the Internet. Due to her extensive health issues, she can't go to school like other children. Her mother drove her out to the wreck site to leave her bear."

"Hmm, well, that killed my lead. Could be someone is using Kee

Kee's name. There was someone outside Slade's door. Your officer was tased?" Slade and Evelyn were alone in her inn. "Slade recognized the voice. He couldn't really place it. Someone familiar from what he heard before he ran for it."

"That's not helpful. Wells could check out who's at the local motels. A name would help."

Donna forgave the man the obvious since his memory had been affected by his attack. A nurse bopped in, looked at the monitors, then at Donna. "Whatever you're talking about is upsetting him."

His blood pressure was spiking. "All right, I'll send in Wells." She kissed him on the forehead and released her grip on his hand. "Get better. I need you."

"Where are you going?"

"Back to the inn, obviously. I left Slade and Princess Anastasia alone."

"What?" His bushy eyes drew together.

"I'll explain later." She debated leaving. Any nurse could take care of him, but would they care as much as she did?

Right now, chaos or possibly murder could be happening at the inn. "I'll sneak in later tonight if I can."

"You will. I have no doubt."

Wells passed her at the door, already summoned. "Keep him calm," she instructed the young patrolman.

"I will, ma'am."

Normally, she'd bark at him to not call her ma'am, but today she didn't have the inclination. Instead, she held her hand up as she walked out to the waiting room. Her family's eyes targeted her, asking what they did not want to verbalize. "He's weak, but stubbornly still working on the case. I need a ride home." Her mother was the first to volunteer.

They walked to the parking lot in silence. Inside of her mother's luxurious sedan, Cecilia was the first to speak.

"You have to tell him how you feel. You'll regret it if you don't." She switched on the ignition, acting as if she did no more than advise Donna not to wear white shoes after Labor Day.

"It's not that easy. Sometimes I don't even know how I feel. Sometimes he can be so sweet. Other times he's as obstinate as a mule. But when I saw him slipping down the wall, my heart stopped."

Her mother reached for her hand and squeezed it. "I understand. Don't let your fears make you miss out on what could be a grand adventure." She retrieved her hand and backed out.

"Maybe. Right now, I have a case to sew up. At least that way, Mark can get some rest."

Her mother, instead of telling her to let the police take care of it as she expected, asked, "Can I help?"

"I'm not sure how."

"Tell me what you know so far. I've always been good at puzzles."

"I guess it can't hurt. You know Summer was shot. Slade was in the car, but wasn't hurt because he was reclining. At first, I thought it was a rabid fan named Kee Kee, but Mark shot that down."

"Anything unusual about the case?"

"I went to the wreck site, which is at a curve in the road. There's also this crumbling barn before the curve. I figured whoever shot Summer hid behind the barn. Of course, they had to know she'd be on the road. I checked her website, and she'd announced her appearance in Legacy. Route 17 is the most direct way unless she flew."

Cecilia drove with a textbook precision Donna had always admired, but slowing down for every stop and looking both ways impinged on the need for speed. "You can pick it up some, Mom."

"I know I can, but I'm thinking about the case. It would be hard to know when Summer would drive by."

"Which means Summer told someone. Slade mentioned hearing someone familiar outside his hospital room door. It could be the same person, but why would she be after him? The most obvious one would be she thought he saw the shooter. So far, he hasn't made much sense. He told me Kee Kee was some intense, slender woman with black hair. Turns out she's an eleven-year-old girl."

Her mother made a slight "Ohh" noise. "It starts to make sense."

Nothing made sense so far. "You act like you know something."

"I might." Ahead of them, a girl on a black motorcycle idled in front of the inn. "Was it her?"

Chapter Twenty-Two

HER MOTHER PULLED out her phone and announced, "I'll get her plate number, and call it in."

After all her hard work, it would be just like her mother to nab a license number and solve the crime. Then again, it was probably kids being kids. "It could be nothing."

"I'll call Betty at the BMV, get her to at least run the tag."

"You do that. I need to get inside to make sure everything is okay."

Donna swung the door open as soon as her mother pulled up behind the bike and reached for her phone. "Wait, I didn't finish my theory."

Her mother's voice faded as she sprinted for the front door, and the bike zoomed off down the street. At the steps, Jasper's frenzied barking penetrated the glass. The interior lights flickered off and on and a long scream ripped through the air. Donna swung the door wide without fully thinking out any plan of attack.

On the foyer floor, surrounded by broken glass, was a girl dressed in black. Jasper circled the girl while emitting a low growl. Every now and then, he'd dart in and nip at her. Donna knew her dog well enough to know he wouldn't draw blood. Slade stood barefooted among the glass shards, bleeding on her oriental runner, with a gun in his hand.

Evelyn, still in her Princess Anastasia dress, swung a heavy candelabrum at the girl, who covered her head with her hands and screamed, "Stop it! You're crazy!"

She rolled away from Evelyn's candelabrum and crab-walked toward the wall yelling, "You're supposed to be dead. If you drove the car like a real man, you'd be done. How was I to know Summer would drive or wear that stupid hat?"

Donna edged her way around Evelyn to Slade. "Is that hers?" she asked of the gun.

"Yeah, she dropped it when Anastasia hit her the first time."

Not liking the lax way he held it, she told him, "Give it to me. I will shoot her, and I'm a good shot." Her assertion might be stretching it, but she could probably bluff better than Slade.

The girl lunged before the gun exchange could take place. Evelyn nailed her with the candelabrum, crying, "That's one for the aristocracy!"

The girl dropped like a bowling ball. Donna checked her pulse, still alive. "Let's tie her up while we can."

Slade knelt beside the downed girl and withdrew his belt to loop it around her wrists. Donna sprinted to the parlor to grab the decorative cord holding back the drapes to bind the culprit's ankles.

"Not sure why Kee Kee would act like this," Slade said. "I thought she was Summer's number-one fan, not a hired killer."

"She isn't Kee Kee." Donna patted the woman down, checking for additional weapons. Enough crime dramas featured the bad guys escaping by using an undetected gun or knife. A square lump in her inside jacket pocket turned out to be a wallet. Inside was a New York driver's license with the name of Traci Warren. She held it up to Slade, who took the proffered license.

"New York, huh. Explains how she could have tailed us." He closed his eyes and exhaled. "This all has been part of a long, convoluted nightmare."

★

THE POLICE ARRIVED while Donna kneeled to pick glass out of Slade's foot. Evelyn was cheerfully singing a foreign song Donna assumed was Russian. The wannabe assassin was hogtied. Slade must have excelled in junior rodeo.

Her mother followed the officers in, escorted by Herman, decked out in a powder blue tuxedo.

"Where have you been?" Donna asked.

Herman replied first. "It's the holidays; I wanted to be suitably dressed." He spotted Evelyn and smiled. "I see you have company."

They both watched Herman move toward the unpredictable Evelyn, who was very primly sitting in a chair with her hands on her lap.

"Look at that, I may have made a match." Her voice became more matter of fact as she turned back to Donna. "I had to catch the killer on the motorcycle."

Jasper gave a slight growl to denote he was watching his prisoner. Donna motioned to the now awake, sullen girl. "This is your killer, Traci, an unstable fan. She was a member of Summer's street team. The female assumed Kee Kee's identity when she met Summer at a recent function. Traci alluded she'd do anything for Summer, including shooting her husband."

The restrained killer snarled at the two of them. "Summer didn't come out and ask me to do it. I suggested it."

"Darn." Her mother narrowed her eyes at the girl. "I must have nailed the accomplice."

An officer nodded in Cecilia's direction. "Bumped would be the more accurate description."

Her mother flushed a little. "Hardly touched her. She overreacted and crashed her bike."

The truth probably resided somewhere in between the two. Donna noticed Wells among the officers. "Hey, good to see you. The trussed-up female confessed all. Summer talked her into killing Slade, not herself, of course. Summer had asked not to be told when the murder would happen so she could be as shocked as everyone else. She must have recognized her on the bike, and that's why she pulled the emergency brake, hoping to buy time. Traci, here, mistook her for Slade and came after him to get even."

Wells cuffed the girl's hands before removing the bonds. "What's the world coming to? She's just a kid."

"A deadly one. That buddy of hers is, too."

"I'll get her out of here, and you can debrief Taber for me."

"I'll do that."

Tennyson, Robert, Maria, and Daniel pulled into the parking lot and watched the departing police cars.

"Mercy," Robert commented, loud enough for her to hear. "This inn is just like being in some reality show. Only more dramatic."

It was hard to be mad at the man when he spoke the truth. "Hope the neighbors enjoyed the show and feel the same way."

"Hard to say." He peered around her into the trashed foyer. "Wow, what happened here?

"A lot. More than what can be explained in a couple of sentences."

Tennyson edged around the broken glass. "You can bet there wouldn't be anything like this going on at my house. The Painted Lady Inn has more action and better food than home."

Donna stooped to pick up a large shard. "I could do with less action." A silent survey revealed overturned furniture, broken glass from a large ornamental vase, pictures askew on the walls, and a dented candelabrum. Most everything was fixable, except for the vase.

"I bet we can all pitch in and make some holiday magic," Robert announced, while giving Tennyson a nudge with his elbow.

"Magic?" Tennyson's eyebrows knitted together. "Got a magic kit for my tenth birthday, but I was never any good at it."

Everyone did help. Donna had to give over the kitchen control to her mother and Maria when she slipped away to visit Mark. She nodded at the nurse on duty as she walked to Mark's room. The staff tended to be more lenient about visiting hours during the holidays. Mark's gruff voice grumbled about something. It would be just like him, trying to sneak a smoke. A few extra-long strides brought her to the doorway. Instead of reaching for a smoke, he was grumbling into his phone.

"It figures. She solved the crime without my help. I'll never hear the end of it."

Donna had to laugh. "It's not a competition."

"Speak of the devil. Thanks for the heads-up."

She fisted one hand on her hip. "I assume it was Wells. I don't appreciate being compared to the devil."

"It's an expression. Besides, Wells wanted to give me a visual with the suspect being trussed up like a calf, you picking glass out of Slade's feet, and your spacy visitor singing to herself."

"That spacey visitor knocked out the killer with a candelabrum. I may have to keep her around in case any other violent fans show up."

"Traci Warren has a long record. Don't make the mistake of thinking she's some misunderstood kid."

Donna pulled the chair closer to the bed. "Trust me. I won't shed any tears over her. She was yelling at Slade for not driving and making her shoot the wrong person. Makes me wonder why Summer just didn't divorce him. He's a little whiny sometimes and not especially bright, but it's hard to say if he always is with the head trauma."

"A two-million-dollar life insurance policy had just been taken out on Slade. Double if he died of unnatural causes. Good chance the man never even signed the papers."

"I don't get it. Summer was famous. She had all these fans."

"Appearances can be deceiving. They don't have a report back on Summer's finances yet, but I'll bet she's broke. Not only would she get a new inflow of cash, but would rid herself of a husband who no longer suited."

The story felt right, even if it had a tragic end. "Near the end, Slade was getting on my nerves, but now I feel sorry for him again. It's a dark day when you find out your spouse wanted someone to kill you."

"Yeah." He used his bent knuckle to rub the space between his eyes. "Slade isn't the only one who's ever heard that unwelcome news. At least he's alive."

"True. Let's talk about something happier. The family is at home scouring the inn for your important presence on Christmas day."

Mark placed his hand over the electrodes on his chest. "Makes me feel like a visiting celebrity."

"You are."

Chapter Twenty-Three

DANIEL WENT TO pick up Mark, giving Donna time to put the final touches on the meal. As children, they could never wait for breakfast before tearing into their presents. She pulled out the smoky grits and sausage casserole from the oven. It smelled wonderful, but probably wouldn't be on Mark's doctor's prescribed diet list that emphasized raw fruits and vegetables. Good chance the man needed to reduce his caffeine intake, too.

The toaster chimed, indicating the chicks in blankets were done. They were a version of pigs in a blanket, but with apples and chicken sausage. Those were for Daniel, who'd loved them as a child. She pulled the beet and citrus salad out of the fridge that might cause Mark to groan until he tasted it. She tried to make everyone's favorites. Her mother popped her head into the kitchen.

"Can I help?"

"Get out the brandy slush. It should be thawed out enough to dip into cups." Her mother heaved the heavy plastic bucket onto the counter near the waiting glasses.

"I should have done that." She often forgot how old her mother was since she always seemed capable. "I'm surprised one of your gentlemen friends didn't want to monopolize you today."

Cecilia gave her head a toss, making the bells on her jaunty holiday cap ring. "I had invitations, but I wanted to be with my family. For later on tonight, I invited Luke over to watch *It's a Wonderful*

Life."

"Luke. That's a new name."

"Pish-posh. I've said it more than once. You weren't listening."

Donna acknowledged it could be a possibility. Tennyson came in the back door with an armful of wood, Loralee and Jasper following on his heels. He took an appreciative sniff. "Yum. Have any of you seen Robert?"

Her mother's eyes danced with hidden knowledge. "It is Christmas. I imagine he's either at the North Pole or soaking up some rays at Key West."

Tennyson laughed as he backed into the interior door. Donna called after him. "Make up the fire in both the parlor and the dining room."

Evelyn peeked into the kitchen. "It's so wonderful to have competent servants."

Her mother waited until her highness had moved on to observe another servant. "Only you would take that woman in. You're a better person than I am."

"Not true."

The bell on the front door jingled, announcing the rest of the guests had arrived. Donna turned off the oven and stepped into the foyer. Daniel tried to help Mark off with his coat, who shrugged off his helping hands. "I can do this."

Donna had to smile. He sounded almost normal. She stepped forward and took his coat to hang in the hall closet. "The cold put some pink in your cheeks. Today, you'll be the guest of honor. Should we have classic holiday jazz, instrumental hymns, or kitschy favorites?"

"Definitely kitschy. Hope you have the one with the dogs barking 'Jingle Bells.'"

"I do. Why don't you sit in the parlor? Tennyson has the fire going, and the tree looks so nice."

Mark held onto her hand. "I'm only sitting if you sit with me."

"I have brunch to put on the table."

Cecilia drifted in with a serving tray with a filled wine glass and a cup of tea on it. "Here." She gave the brandy slush to Donna. Cecilia gave Mark a sweet smile. "I know you'll drink this green tea just for me since I made it for you."

"You Tollhouse women don't play fair."

Her mother's laughter floated behind her. Maria grinned and pushed a wrapped box under the tree. "I'll turn on the music and get the food on the table. You two relax."

Donna perched on the edge of the matching wing chair. "I'm not sure I know how to relax."

"You need to learn." He sipped the tea and put it down with a surprised expression. "This isn't bad."

"Glad you think so. I read your medical recommendations. You need to switch out coffee for green tea."

At his frown, she softened the blow. "At least half the time and consider decaffeinated."

"Not worth drinking. What were you doing looking at my records? Isn't there a law against that?"

Donna refused to answer, knowing she'd incriminated herself. Instead, she stood, holding out her free hand. "Food's ready."

They crowded around the table decorated with tiny pine trees and crystal angels. Only once a year did she get out her holiday china that depicted a sleigh carrying a family through the snow. The candles shimmered softly on the server. Evelyn summed up her own feelings. Two twin tears slid down her withered cheeks. "I've stepped into a holiday dream. Thank you. So much better than the scrawny tree and pressed turkey loaf."

"Aw," Herman lifted his glass. "Here's to a wonderful holiday and better company." The glasses clinked softly.

Evelyn's remark had her considering the next year. Maybe she could bring Christmas to the nursing home. Her mother encouraged people to eat up, but when the grandfather clock bonged twice she stood up. "It's time to retire to the parlor."

Donna's curiosity was piqued as to why her mother wanted to hurry everyone along before they even had dessert. She played along. If innkeeping taught her nothing else, it taught her to go with the flow. Donna had gifts for everyone. Her almost-famous guest had already left with his manager, who would be able to put a good PR spin on everything.

Evelyn acted normal again, which might make her gift inappropriate but she'd give it to her anyhow. She'd seen it in the front window of the costume store. Donna picked out the beribboned package and handed it to Evelyn.

"For me?" She pressed her thin hand against her neck before ripping into the package. The tissues separated to reveal a rich emerald velvet cloak. Evelyn arched her neck regally. "You have outdone yourself. We are well pleased."

The princess was back. Her mother reached around the tree to pull out a smaller box and handed it to Tennyson. "Robert asked me to give you this."

He shook the box, which rattled. Only a ribbon held it closed. Inside were keys and a title. "He left me his truck. I can't believe it. It's exactly what I need."

Mark leaned toward Donna. "You told me a girlfriend."

"Santa knows best."

Maria pushed a box to her husband with a secret smile. Daniel lifted the top to reveal a bright yellow shirt that had written in primary colors *Best Daddy in the World.*

Daniel held it up and stared at it for a few seconds before gazing at his wife, who gave a small head bob and grinned. Cecilia whooped, then proceeded to dance an Irish jig.

Mark's hoarse laughter made Donna reach for the gift she'd made for him. It was heavy so she held it with two hands." It's not taped so you can just lift the lid off. I'm thinking maybe I should take it back."

"I should at least get to see my own present before you exchange it." His hands joined hers on the box. "Give it up. It's mine now."

Her fingers released the box as she watched him open the lid. His face brightened as he lifted the lid. "It is a Merry Christmas." He tilted the box enough for the others to see, but not too much that it would cause the oversized caramel cheesecake to slide out.

Maria made an appreciative murmur. "Ooh, nice."

Her mother leaned forward and gestured to the sweet dessert. "Donna only bakes for those she cares about."

Apparently, her mother had missed out on all the strangers parading through the inn or assumed she cared about them much more than she did. "Mom."

"Wait." Mark held up his hand. "Didn't have time to shop for a real present, but I have a proclamation to read." He pulled a scrolled paper out of his shirt pocket and cleared his throat. "On this day, December 25, 2016, I declare that I, Mark Taber, have stopped smoking. I have thrown away all cigarettes, cigarillos, cigars, and lighters. I give Donna Tollhouse permission to monitor my progress even when it involves poking, prodding, and even the dreaded nagging."

Daniel yelped at the last one. "You asked for it."

Mark went to put the paper back in his pocket, but she snatched it up. Her eyes raced over the words, the ones he didn't read. "What's this about always having sweet breath, the better for kissing?"

Mark's face heated. "I thought I'd read that later."

Tennyson clapped his hands. "Kiss. Kiss."

Daniel joined in, as did Maria and even Cecilia.

Evelyn pushed herself up, arranged her cape around her shoulders, and held out an index finger at Mark. "It is my royal decree. You kiss my faithful servant."

Mark stood, more than a little embarrassed. Donna grabbed his hand and pulled him out of the room.

"Make it good," Daniel yelled.

The two of them slipped into the dining room where they wrapped their arms around each other. Donna snuggled into Mark's shoulder. "You don't even smell like smoke."

He choked on whatever he might have been about to say and then cleared his throat. "New clothes, your brother suggested it, he picked them out, and brought them to the hospital. Told me I'd need a new car, too, if I want to woo his sister."

"Hmm, sounds good. This has been a crazy Christmas for me with my old fiancé showing up with a family in tow. Tennyson said something about Christmas Past. Let's say I'm not sorry to let that particular memory fade."

Mark brushed a kiss on her hair. "I'm more interested in Christmas Present."

"Me, too." She turned her lips up to meet his. It felt like magic. Christmas magic.

A tall man shimmered in the corner beside an angelic being. "I'm glad I got to see that, but I do want to be back for my grandchild's arrival into the world."

"Demand, demand, you Tollhouses are all alike."

The End

Recipe Backstory

These recipes are not Donna's concoction, but came from my grandmother. My grandmother taught herself how to cook since she married at 15. She was also a young widow who made a living by cooking pies, cakes, and cookies for the local bakery. Often, people would ask her for her recipes. Always polite, she did give them a recipe with important ingredients missing. Baking was how she supported her children. When people asked about any extra ingredients, she told them with a sweet smile the secret ingredient was love. As family members, we inherited the entire recipes. Enjoy.

Family Favorite Sugar Cookies

Ingredients
- 1 c. butter
- 1 c. vegetable oil
- 1 c. sugar
- 1 c. powdered sugar
- 1 tsp. vanilla
- 2 med to large eggs
- 4 ½ c. flour
- 1 tsp baking soda
- ½ tsp salt

Mix together butter, oil, and sugars. Add eggs and vanilla. Gradually add flour mixture. Roll into walnut sized balls (ping-pong size), roll in sugar, and place on an ungreased cookie sheet. Bake 375 degrees for 8 to 10 minutes or until light brown.

Recipe Backstory

My mother worked long hours as a nurse. (Bet you can guess where part of my inspiration for Donna came from.) As a single parent, she depended on the crockpot to fix dinner. Here's one of her crockpot recipes. It's great for company.

Crockpot Company Turkey

First, you'll need a 6-quart crockpot.

Ingredients
- 1 (6-9) lb. boneless turkey breast
- 1 oz. packet of dry onion soup mix
- ¾ c. water
- 1 onion, diced
- 2 tbsp. garlic powder
- 1 tbsp. onion powder
- 1 tbsp. dried parsley
- 1 tbsp. seasoned salt
- 1 tbsp. dried oregano
- 1 tbsp. dried basil

Directions
1. Place turkey breast, breast side up in the crockpot.
2. Assemble the additional ingredients in a bowl, then mix, pour over the turkey. Cook on high for 1 hour, then lower temperature to low for an additional 6-7 hours. When turkey breast registers 165 degrees, it's done.

Holiday Brandy Slush

This is what Mark Taber didn't get to drink at Christmas.

Ingredients
- 5 cups boiling water
- 4 individual green tea bags
- 1 c. white sugar
- 16 oz. can of frozen OJ
- 2 c. of brandy
- 1 2L bottle of Sprite or similar lemon lime soda
- 16 oz. can of frozen lemonade

Directions
1. Steep tea in 2 cups boiling water for 10 minutes. Place remaining 3 cups boiling water in a 9x13 inch pan. Stir in sugar until dissolved. Stir in lemonade concentrate, orange juice concentrate, and brandy. Remove tea bags and stir tea into mixture. Freeze overnight.
2. To serve, scoop the desired amount into a glass, then fill glass with lemon-lime soda, and stir.

Make Ahead Cinnamon Raisin Muffins

These also freeze well to make ahead. Freeze them in a single layer in a cake pan with a cover. Let them come to room temperature on their own as opposed to defrosting them in the microwave.

Ingredients

Muffins
- ¾ c. raisins
- 1 & ¾ c flour
- 2 & ½ tsp baking powder
- ½ tsp salt
- ½ tsp ground cinnamon
- ½ c light brown sugar
- ¼ c granulated sugar
- 1/3 c unsalted butter, melted
- 1 large egg, room temperature
- 1 tsp vanilla extract
- ¾ c whole milk, room temperature

Topping
- 2 tbsp. Light brown sugar
- ½ tsp ground cinnamon

Instructions

1. Bring 3 c. of water to a boil in a saucepan. Remove from heat and add raisins. Let sit for 10 minutes. Drain well and set aside.
2. Preheat oven to 400°F. Spray a 12-cup muffin pan with cooking spray or line with paper liners; set aside.
3. In a large mixing bowl, combine the flour, baking powder, salt, cinnamon, and sugars. Stir with a whisk to combine. Make a well in the center.
4. In a 4 c. measuring cup with a pour spout whisk the butter, egg, vanilla, and milk together until well blended. Pour into the center of the flour mixture. Fold everything together until just moistened. Avoid over-mixing. Fold in the raisins. Excessive stirring toughens the muffin and ruins the rounded top.
5. Divide the batter among the prepared muffin cups. Mix the cinnamon and sugar for the topping together in a small bowl and sprinkle it over the batter in muffin cup. Bake for 18 to 20 minutes or until a toothpick inserted into the center comes out clean.
6. Transfer muffins to a wire rack to cool completely.

Death Pledges a Sorority

A GIRLS' WEEKEND had been Maria's brainchild. She'd come up with the idea and helped Donna shake down local merchants and restaurants for two-for-one coupons to stick in the participants' goodie bags along with chocolate, hand cream, and individual size bottles of wine. Mainly it was Maria's doing, since Donna still hadn't perfected her welcoming innkeeper banter yet. The same time her first fully booked girls' weekend was about to happen, her brother had decided to whisk her sister-in-law away for a romantic trip before the two became three. Most people might call it thoughtful. Her eyes narrowed as she realized she might have even suggested it. Still, did he have to pick this weekend when Donna desperately needed help?

The bell on the front door jingled. Guests already? A familiar voice called out. "Mother's here to save the day!" Her smiling parent entered the kitchen, carrying a bulging bag. She placed the colorful tote on the counter and hugged Donna.

"Hi." Her mother showing up was never a simple *I was in the neighborhood* type of thing. "So, what merits the pleasure of your company?"

Her mother laughed and gave her a playful slap. "You act like you don't know."

She didn't. "I should know?" Her eyebrows arched in inquiry.

"Silly." Her mother smirked at her. "There you go teasing me. I never thought you ever had much of a sense of humor as a child, but you must have picked up some. Maria called me on her way out of town. She told me you needed a hand with your activities."

"Ah," Donna stalled as she searched her memory for any hints that her mother might be assisting her this weekend. Maria had apologized profusely, promising to get someone to help. She'd expected one of Maria's co-workers who would have been easy to boss around, not her mother. "It's all coming back now."

"Good thing I'm here since your memory's slipping." Cecilia turned and grabbed her bag from the counter. "You can thank me later for the fun items I brought. At least one of us has a clue how to party."

She wasn't going to respond to the dig. She knew how to party; it just usually involved a food processor, possibly a blender, heavy cream, and top shelf brandy. "What do you have?"

"Fun!" Her mother pulled a can from the bag and sprayed into the air.

The stink of aerosol and a shot of color, then something gooey plopped onto the floor. Donna stared at the color blob in disgust. Tennyson strolled into the room as Cecilia pushed the nozzle down again.

"Silly string. Way cool, Cici."

When had he started calling her mother Cici? That was supposed to be a dating name to keep her rejected suitors from tracking her down. There wasn't time to query anyone about name changes when her hardwood floors were in danger. "Not cool. It will ruin my floors. Besides, I think that would appeal more to fifth grade boys than grown women."

Her mother's gleeful expression drooped a little. "You could be right. The employee who suggested it was a teen." She turned the can over in her hand and stared at it. "I can't even read what it has in it. Probably better off not using it. Here, Ten, you take it."

The lanky college senior stepped back a few steps and held his hands. "Appreciate the generosity, but I'm trying to turn over a more serious leaf."

Donna looked up from a kneeling position on the floor as she cleaned up the fun fallout. "There's something more serious than philosophy?"

"There is." Tennyson's shoulders went back as he straightened up to his full height. "Business."

"Ah." Cecilia nodded and gave him an approving smile. "Business can be very serious. Good for you."

Did anyone miss the fact that Tennyson had spent almost four years in school? "What about all the time you already spent in school?"

"It's all cool. My credits transfer. The philosophy classes can be electives. Emily thinks it's the right thing to do."

Donna stood, grateful that Tennyson wasn't her son. She wasn't too sure how she handled the announcement. As an employer and amateur sleuth, her attention caught on one word. "Emily?" There usually was a female involved in Tennyson's major decisions.

"Yeah, she's a business major, too. Very smart. Maybe I could bring her around and she could give you advice on making the inn more profitable."

Her mother had already overloaded her with articles she clipped out of journals that she thought Donna could benefit from reading. "I'd love to meet her."

"Me, too," Cecilia piped in.

"Great. I'll tell Emily. What are you planning?"

Before Donna could answer her mother did. "Girls weekend." She pushed the bag to its side and started pulling out wildly colored objects.

Donna's voice grew higher with each word. "Tell me those aren't water guns, bubbles, and lipstick tubes?"

Cecilia gestured to the objects as if a game show hostess. "I told you I knew how to party."

Obviously, it had been a long time since her mother had been to a party or the events at the senior center were being planned by a ten year old. "Come on, Mom. If the silly string would ruin the floor, what would the water guns do the walls, carpets, or the furniture?"

Her mother snorted and leaned against the counter. "You're a class A party pooper. No wonder you never had any slumber parties."

"We didn't have slumber parties because Dad didn't want a bunch of girls running up and down the stairs squealing while he was trying to sleep."

"Okay, that may have been true."

The hall phone rang forcing Donna to run to get it before it stopped, leaving her mother and Tennyson discussing the possibility of a water gun fight outside in January. "Hello. The Painted Lady Inn. How can I help you?"

There was silence on the other end, some light breathing, not enough to be an obscene phone call, but just enough to let her know a live person was at the other end. Then, whoever it was hung it up. *Wrong number.* Still, she placed the phone back in the cradle and stared at it. An ominous chill teased the back of her neck.

"People call wrong numbers all the time." She returned to the kitchen in time to hear Tennyson's summation of Girls' Weekend.

"I don't know about writing on people's faces with lipstick when they're asleep. I thought women went away together to drink too much, eat all the foods they normally avoided, talk about what celebrity they'd like to be with on a deserted island, and watch romantic comedies."

"Me, too." She agreed, hoping to dissuade her mother from her childish pranks. "They might work in a massage, mani pedi, or do some shopping. Legacy has some excellent boutiques."

Her mother threw her hands up. "No one knows how to have fun anymore. I guess the board games I have in the car are a no-go, too."

With any luck, her mother didn't bring any exclusively children's games. "Bring them in. We'll put them somewhere in the dining room in full view so if people want to play, they can."

"We'll need a sign." Cecilia opened drawers looking for a pen and paper. Once she found supplies, she constructed a note. "Tennyson, will you go get the games out of my car. Backseat."

"No problem." He headed out the side door at a half jog.

It wasn't fair that energy tended to be wasted on the young. Donna slid closer to her mother who was intent on writing in fancy script. "You aren't writing anything about you're a party pooper if you don't play the games."

"Of course not." Cecilia held up her carefully lettered sign. TAKE YOUR FUN UP TO THE NEXT LEVEL!

Not as bad as she thought, but the guests might think some fee was involved, too. "Couldn't you put something such as feel free to use?"

"I could, but…"

They both glanced as Tennyson ran into the room. "Hey, there's someone lurking in the bushes beside the house."

"What?" Donna pushed past Tennyson to reach the door.

Her mother's voice reached her as she stepped on the stoop. "Wait, it could be dangerous. Call the police."

It was barely eleven on a sunny day in a good neighborhood. What could be dangerous? No one visible in the parking lot unless they were hiding behind the cars. The evergreen bushes might provide some cover, but not enough since Tennyson spotted whoever it was, probably kids. Donna hesitated on the step, wondering if she should have brought something out with her. She opened the door and yelled back into the house. "Send out Jasper."

Her aging puggle's main skill was snapping treats out of the air, but he was a good scent hound. The clatter of dog nails signaled her pooch's location. The dog came out on the stoop followed by Tennyson who had two cans of silly string with his index fingers resting on the nozzle. Her mother followed with two squirt guns. She tried to hand one to Donna.

"I don't think a lime green squirt gun will fool anyone." Instead of taking the offered gun, she knelt beside her dog and pointed toward the bushes. "Squirrel. Go find."

The dog began baying before his short legs propelled him off the porch and across the gravel driveway. He skirted the bushes and even managed to wiggle through them. He stopped his search, and gave Donna a questioning glance. Could be her dog figured out he'd been had.

A cold breeze reminded her that she'd darted out without her jacket. Her hands chafed her arms as she slowly moved down the steps. "Where did you see the trespasser?"

Tennyson pointed to where Jasper stood staring back at them. No one there now. "What was the person wearing? Did you notice if our visitor was male or female?"

"Ah, the person had a dark hoodie on and was half squatting, trying to hide behind the bushes." He placed the cans he was holding on the stoop and moved to stand beside her.

Cecilia pushed her way between the two of them. "A dark hood-ie. That must mean a burglar. Burglars always wear hoodies."

There probably wasn't a dress code for the felonious population. Before she could point this out, Tennyson did with a touch more patience than she would have.

"Most of the guys on campus have dark hoodies and some of the girls too. Although, the girls tend to favor brighter colors."

"True," she found herself agreeing, aware that the spotted could be one of the thousand students who attended Legacy University. More likely, it was that annoying teen who claimed he was a press member and pushed his way onto her lawn when a dead body showed up in her inn's top most parlor.

"Too cold for me." Cecilia turned and went up the steps. Tennyson headed off to the car to retrieve the board games he'd forgotten. Donna called after him.

"Make sure you lock the car."

Her mother might argue she'd never locked her car, but it looked like times were changing.

Author Notes

- If you liked this tale, make sure you check out the entire series including **Murder Mansion, Drop Dead Handsome, Killer Review,** and **Christmas Calamity. Death Pledges a Sorority** comes out in early 2017, followed by **Caribbean Catastrophe** in February.
- Follow M K Scott on Amazon to keep track of the latest books and upcoming series.
- Check out the website www.morgankwyatt.com to sign up for the newsletter and information about contests and prizes.
- Looking for romantic comedies, romantic mysteries or sweet romance; check out Morgan K Wyatt.
- Remember the best way to encourage an author is to write a review.
- Thanks for reading this and have a wonderful day.

M. K. Scott

Made in the USA
Middletown, DE
18 October 2022